TEXAS TALL

SHORT STORIES

© 2021 Mike Lowrie. All rights reserved. No part of this book may be scanned, copied, uploaded or reproduced in any form or by any means, photographically, electronically or mechanically, without written permission from the copyright holder.

ISBN: 978-1-943492-90-9 (Hardback)
ISBN: 978-1-943492-91-6 (Soft Cover)

Book design by designpanache

llustrations by Mick J. Prodger

ELM GROVE PUBLISHING

San Antonio, Texas, USA
www.elmgrovepublishing.com

Elm Grove Publishing is a legally registered trade name of Panache Communication Arts, Inc.

TEXAS TALL

SHORT STORIES

MIKE LOWRIE

Contents

Introduction

Good writers have one common denominator with each other. They must be good storytellers first. The Texas storyteller is already world famous for taking a simple story and embellishing it to ridiculousness, but that's the art. And embellishing is the weapon of choice.

Most of the short stories written about early Texas are of the western frontier type. Tales of the Texas Rangers, cattle drives, Comanche problems, and the fight for independence fill the shelves in Texas libraries.

I decided very early on in this project that if I wrote another book about the Texas frontier, it would end up being just another book on the shelf. Instead, I decided to write about Texas people and incidents, all occurring in the twenty-first century.

All of the following stories are fictional, but all began from an element of absolute truth. That's right, each story has a factual basis to it. The other 90 percent of the stories have been smartly embellished. That's my literary right as a writer.

The most exciting aspect for me in writing this book was that these collections are very unique. I purposely did not follow the norms or the rules that other writers do, all the time having my characters stand alone among situational unpredictabilities. There are no stories like them.

★

I have led with the first short story, *The Piano Tuner.* It is the story of a blind piano tuner and the influence he had on the lives of the people he touched. Without getting too far in depth, the reader might want to know this interesting backstory.

In 1972, my family moved to San Antonio. My mother was insistent on getting her piano tuned, fearing the move had skewed the tones. After a few phone calls, a blind piano tuner came to see us one day. I was so impressed with his skills, I evidently never forgot. Over forty-five years later, I put the memory to a story.

Good Deeds is a historical fiction piece that centers around Hurricane *Ike* when it hit Galveston Island and the Bolivar Peninsula. The story is about three young black kids and how the two older brothers are forced to take measures into their own hands.

The most questionable story I have ever written is the third short story, *Texas Clam Bake*. It is about a lesbian biker gang that is stalked and terrorized by a giant bisexual woman from Poland.

What started out as a humorous story, was quickly quashed by my straight test readers.

My top reader told me, "The first lesbian biker gang that comes through here will assassinate you." So I put it away and didn't think about it for months.

When I did think on it again, I reread it and told myself, "This is a good story. I'm going to get another opinion." Shortly after, I contacted a lesbian friend of mine and asked her if she would read it. After she gave me the thumbs up, I put *Texas Clam Bake* back on the market. It has been lesbian approved.

She's No Barbie is an idea I came up with to give some insight on the South Texas area. The setting is in a fictional town, a short distance from the Mexican border. I try to paint a picture of the harshness of this land, being so close to the border, and a *gringa* adjusting to a Spanish-speaking environment. The real people I knew that lived there lost countless dogs and cats to everything from rattlesnakes to coyotes.

I will be declining to give the reader insight on *The Fishing Trip*. Although this is a humorous piece, it still deals with subjects that may be judged and scrutinized by some. There are elements of truth to this story, but if you want to find out what they are, you'll have to ask me in person.

It was on a cold moonlit night when four hunters and one boy stood around a campfire, trying to keep themselves warm. They had been hunting all day and everyone was fairly tired. After someone broke out a bottle of whiskey, they started telling stories about their hunts and other adventures.

The boy was spellbound by their stories, becoming transfixed by the dangers they faced and inspired by the self-proclaimed acts of bravery they told.

As time passed, the boy attempted to retell the stories to his friends, but the inevitable erosion of the tales over time caused him to forget details in some stories and add in others. So he learned how to embellish, and his stories became better.

At school, the boy developed a habit of daydreaming. Always looking out the window instead of to his studies, he fought grizzly bears in his imagination, floated on the clouds above, and saved the girl of his dreams from certain peril.

That boy became a storyteller. And his first story was about a blind piano tuner.

"If I couldn't tell these stories, I think my head would explode."

Mike Lowrie
mikeent@earthlink.net

The Piano Tuner

It is said that the most beautiful sounds to the human ear actually echo throughout the realms of heaven. They are divine harmonies, a continuous chorus sung by suspended angels and broadcasting from the gates to the throne. It is also said that the few mortals privileged to have heard this holy music are stunned in awe, never being able to fully describe the perfections.

I'd like to think that we do our part here on Earth, for many times the Alamo City Orchestra has enticed my emotions to shed tears from a romance and my heartbeat to run away during a chase.

Located in the historic city of San Antonio, the orchestra prides itself in the classical as most other symphonies do, but they also cater to pop, jazz, or anything that presents the quality format. The players in the orchestra dream big, practice diligently, and they deliver within the acoustics of the great Sequin Hall. I've discovered that a good orchestra can create a spiritual festival, prompting astute listeners into unexplored imaginations and warming their souls.

I am their biggest fan. I am the bookkeeper.

The turning point began on a particular day of a typical rehearsal. The orchestra was perfecting the power of Beethoven.

Our conductor was Mark Chastain, a graduate of Julliard and of the accelerated programs for conducting orchestras. I, for one, was grateful we acquired Mark. He was a good hire for the money and was exactly who the director wanted, extensive in knowledge and qualifications.

We acquired him at a time when conductors were few to be found. You might say the world had a shortage that year. That and the bigger names that were available wanted to go to big cities like New York. That's where the conductors were praised and venerated with fame, and of course the pay was considerably higher. The truth was that not many up-and-coming conductors chose a city like San Antonio as their first choice, thinking it more as a societal outpost.

That year the local critics summed up Mark's performances as "adequate but uneventful." The entertainment press often wrote that he appeared to be stiff when he conducted, adhering more to the precision of the beat than the melody. It was a minor problem.

Our director sat in the middle of the third row from the back. His name was Reginal Wallace, and he was an expert at two things: classical music and food.

Before Reginal became the director of the Alamo City Orchestra he was a professional clarinet player. Then he discovered the wonderful Mexican food in San Antonio and he bloomed. He became a jolly large man in time, barrel-chested, short stubby fingers, and always a cigar in hand, whether lit or unlit.

As Mark Chastain conducted the orchestra, he suddenly pulled them to a halt then began to instruct them on the intricacies of the piece. It was a normal day of rehearsal.

That's about the time when two people walked in from the foyer and down the aisle towards the stage. It was the blind piano tuner, Nigel Ledger, being led arm in arm by Maria Cisneros, a famous retired opera singer. Both were in their seventies.

It was fascinating to watch people's faces every time they walked in, because they looked like royalty. They looked important. Everyone knew who they were, but few actually knew them personally.

Maria Cisneros was a renowned opera singer during the seventies and eighties. She performed in every major concert hall across the globe and thusly made her mark on the profession. As the working years went by, one day she realized her voice was strained and could no longer hit the high notes. So she bought a large plantation-type house in her hometown of San Antonio and retired.

Nigel Ledger was a different story. He spoke English with a slight Slavic accent and was a mystery to everyone at the symphony except Mark Chastain. It turned out, there was a lot that Mark knew but never told anyone.

Rumor had it that when he was in his thirties, Nigel was in Palermo, Italy composing and conducting with some of the greats of our time when he lost his sight to a mysterious and bad fever.

He was easy to spot in a crowd. Not because he carried a cane or wore dark sunglasses wherever he went, but because he had a Stalin styled mustache and a wild head of hair, like Albert Einstein on a bad hair day.

As the blind are limited in professions, it is not uncommon for those with musical backgrounds to become piano tuners. Nigel Ledger could play the piano in his sleep. His forte was his keen ear for tones, and yet he tuned the piano with intentional imperfections, making it perfect to the human ear. That's why he tuned pianos. That's why he tuned the house piano.

Nigel and Maria's relationship was what one would call tightly confidential. No one really knew what they were to each other. They kept their lives private. All we knew was that once a week they would march down the aisle together towards the stage, like some duke and duchess arriving at a Queen's Ball.

I think their relationship had more to do with keeping each other company than anything else. It stood to reason that they had more in common with each other than they did with the younger generation.

As Mark was speaking to the orchestra, one of the players on the front row told him that the piano tuner was here. Mark promptly had everyone take thirty minutes while Maria escorted Nigel to the piano.

As Nigel sat down at the piano, Maria opened it up and Nigel pulled out his tuning hammer. Then, note by note, he played the keys, tilted his head, and found his tone.

Once satisfied, he played various chords intensely. Only a master tuner would know what he was doing. Meticulously listening to each cord, Nigel was looking for unobstructed pathways through which his harmonies could reach the human heart.

As Nigel played his chords, the orchestra players gradually walked back on stage and took their seats. Mark Chastain took notice and, keeping his eye on Nigel, stepped up on the podium and tapped his baton on the stand to get Nigel's attention. Nigel heard it and paused.

"Nigel, do you know what day it is?"

"Wednesday!" Nigel called back.

"Wednesday yes, but a little bird named Maria… told me that today is your birthday."

On Mark's cue the entire orchestra stood and sang *Happy Birthday* to him. Nigel laughed in excitement then spontaneously raised his hands, conducting the remainder of the song while Maria and Mark sang along.

As I walked down the aisle toward them, they were cheering and clapping, overacting with praise. Although no one really knew him, everyone loved him just as he was, Nigel the piano tuner. The shouts of bravos and encores from the players indicated that they were having fun, something that didn't occur enough.

I hated to interrupt them, but there was business to attend to and Mark was part of it. I called to him, "Mark!"

He turned around, "Hammond?"

"I'm sorry, but we require your presence… in the office if you would?"

"Yes. I'll be right there." Then he walked over to Nigel and put his baton in Nigel's hand, "Nigel. Conduct anything you want. The orchestra knows what to do. Happy Birthday."

Mark and I walked off the stage to the office.

Maria took ahold of Nigel's arm and slowly escorted him to the podium. Nigel stood there for a moment as the orchestra slowly sat down. You could tell he was thinking. After a moment he tapped his baton on the stand and softly said, "*Lohengrin*, Prelude to Act III."

There was a notable gasp heard throughout the players. They didn't expect him to choose such an advanced piece. After all, they thought, he was only a piano tuner.

Nevertheless, they changed their sheet music.

Nigel raised his baton and started Wagner's *Lohengrin* like it was an attack, surely to stun the listener. That's the way Nigel visualized it. It had been forty years since he had conducted anything, and that was back when he could see.

The orchestra immediately saw that his method of conducting was fundamentally different, yet commanding in nature. They followed his baton, and discovered they could read his body movements with ease.

Reginal Wallace was sitting in his office chair when we walked in and took our seats.

"Okay. What's this all about?" Mark asked.

"We're running out of money. That's what," I told them.

"How can that be?" Mark asked.

Reginal spoke up, "Oh come on. You're probably overreacting. All day long you stare at numbers. That can't be good for your brain."

"I wish I was." I continued, "The truth is that we can probably squeak by this year, but unless we have a good finish, it'll be impossible to get any kind of financing for the next year."

Mark placed his hands over his face, "Oh god. This can't be happening. The annual fandango is next week. If word of this gets out, there will be a million questions."

I tried to calm Mark down, "I think you're being a little premature with all the freaking out."

"Hammond! When someone yells, 'The ship is sinking,' people start jumping ship! That's the way people are."

Reginal raised his hand with the unlit cigar between his fingers and gestured, "Everyone needs to calm down"—leaning back in his chair and putting a cigar in his mouth—"God will provide."

So I told him, "Well, I hope so because the devil is going to be at the fandango."

Mark asked, "You mean the chairman?"

"Yes, with all his demon board members," I replied.

Reginal reacted, "Oh shit! We better come up with something, and quick."

When Lohengrin was finished, the orchestra was obviously pumped. They applauded Nigel's performance and began to chatter with each other.

The principle violinist, a girl named Heather, couldn't help but ask, "Mister... Piano Tuner? I think you've done this before."

"I was not always a piano tuner. Please, call me Nigel," He replied. "Is Mr. Chastain still in the office?"

The violinist answered, "Apparently so."

★

We were brainstorming in the office to come up with a solution.

"We've had four visiting performances cancel last year," I tried to explain to them. "That had a lot to do with it. Now we need a gimmick or something to get out of this slump."

"A gimmick?" Mark asked, "Like a dancing bear or dog act?"

"Come on!" I pleaded, "You know what I'm talking about."

Reginal raised his cigar in gesture, "It takes me almost an entire year of preparation to host a visiting entertainer."

I had to reiterate the problem, "Which brings me back to our original problem. This year is too late to get something new and spectacular, but if we don't make it through this year, next year is questionable."

Well, that did it. It looked like I had forced everyone into a corner. There were no quick remarks to this problem, so no one said a word. We just looked at each other, waiting for a new idea to pop out while the orchestra played in the background.

Reginal cocked his head and tried to listen, "Who's conducting the orchestra?"

"The piano tuner," Mark said.

Since Mark Chastain was still in his meeting and the orchestra was still waiting, they insisted that Nigel conduct another piece. When he picked *Summon the Heroes* by John Williams, one of the flute players asked him if he knew the piece by heart, assuming that was the only way it could've been since he was blind.

Nigel pointed the baton towards his head, "Yes. I know the works by heart. I visualize the music... and I orchestrate the works in my head...note by note, from flutes to trumpets to violins to drums. I can hear the intricacies of the harmonies. I can tell who's off-key. You might say my hearing is three times the common man's since I lost my sight."

"So, no offense, but... are you totally blind? Is everything dark?" Linda, the principle celloist asked.

Nigel pointed his baton straight up in the air, "Ah! That is the question, isn't it? I can detect a slight degree of movement. I see the movements of your bows, but not much more. Everything is extremely blurry at all distances. I cannot even say whether you are man or woman, until you speak."

"I'm sorry I asked," apologized Linda.

"Please. Do not be sorry," replied Nigel. "This is my blessing. The only thing I cannot do is see your smiling faces."

There were five seconds of silence. All the players were hanging on every word Nigel was saying. He had captivated the orchestra with his story.

Then standing tall, with an abrupt sweep of his baton to the ready position, Nigel instructed, "'Summon the Heroes!'"

The orchestra plunged into "Summon the Heroes." It was evident that they were having fun again, and now with a new perspective.

Mark, Reginal, and myself were watching our piano tuner conduct, and we were amazed. His movements were a dance, perfectly attuned to the rhythm. It was like a revelation to a question we had not the wit to ask. And yet the answer for all of us was uniformly the same, 'So this is what it's supposed to look like.'

"He's fantastic," I said.

Mark stared at the orchestra. "I've got an idea for you, Reginal."

I'm sure everyone was thinking the same thing at the same time. Nigel Ledger as the guest blind conductor? That wouldn't be a first. There had been others before, but only a handful in history.

Mark dismissed the orchestra early that day, but made sure that Nigel and Maria stayed. As both of them sat on the piano bench, we ran the idea by them.

Reginal started, "Nigel. We would like to know if you would make some guest appearances as conductor."

Maria's mouth opened, "Are you serious?"

"Yes, we're serious," Mark said. "You've still got what it takes, Nigel. I think you would be a wonderful addition to our regular programing."

Nigel just sat there shocked, staring into emptiness. Nigel wanted to accept immediately, but because of his age and disability, he knew he would need special considerations.

Maria looked at Nigel, then looked at us, and then back at him, "Nigel, how do you feel about this?"

Nigel paused and then asked, "If I were to accept, could I make some small conditions?"

"Sure you can, Nigel," Mark replied.

"First, Maria will always lead me to my mark. Secondly, no more than four pieces per performance... and third, I can choose?" He asked cautiously.

Reginal may have been the director and was by definition the one that chose, but Nigel was a master. "Why sure, Mr. Ledger."

"Then I accept your offer."

Reginal smiled and grabbed his hand to shake, "Good. We've got a deal. This is very exciting."

Nigel raised his index finger, "For this year only."

"That will be fine," Reginal gladly accepted.

In business, you might call this a calculated risk; trusting a blind man to carry the symphony to a successful season, or maybe not. There was also a secondary risk. Reginal was not going to notify the Board of Directors about this sudden programing change until the very last moment. The plan was to avoid the board members until they saw it in the billing: "Nigel Ledger, The Blind Conductor." We assumed that Nigel would be on board.

Two days later Maria and Nigel showed up with his music requests. We all talked it over and made preparations for the first concert, which was in two weeks. The first theme was to be a set of Mexican classics. The second themed set would be twentieth-century composers. The last theme would be the lesser-known works of great films.

The plan was for Mark Chastain to conduct four pieces and then introduce Nigel to the audience. Nigel would conduct three to four pieces and then Mark would finish the night.

The entire three programs would finish the season and the year. That would take about four months.

I thought the plan was good. All we had to do was draw the crowd, and Reginal took care of that by contacting every school in the area with a music program to tell them what we were about to do.

The orchestra practiced for one week under Nigel. These were enthusiastic rehearsals for the players. Nigel had a way with speaking that kept everyone's attention. During rehearsals and before every piece of music, Nigel would describe a scene or picture in life that the music could play to. That was his secret weapon that he used to motivate the orchestra.

Maria was Nigel's constant companion and support mechanism. When he would conduct, sometimes I would see her place her hand over her mouth and fight back the tears. She was very proud of him, and I'd like to think that somewhere in their private lives she loved him.

On opening night, Reginal managed to get about seventy-five percent of the seats filled. Half of the seats filled were from schools with music programs. This was all good considering no one knew or had even heard of Nigel Ledger.

The fact that he was being billed as "The Blind Conductor," we were afraid would have a novelty effect and run cold after some time. But we kept our fingers crossed and hoped for the best. Seventy-five percent was good.

Mark Chastain came on stage and conducted pieces from Beethoven, Brahms, and Mendelssohn. Then he turned around on the podium and addressed the audience.

"Ladies and gentlemen. Tonight we have and rare and special treat. It gives me great pleasure to introduce to you, someone who has been the piano tuner for the Alamo City Orchestra for many years. He is not just a piano tuner but a master of the musical arts, and we are very fortunate to have him. Maestro Nigel Ledger!"

Maria escorted Nigel across the stage and up onto the podium as the crowd applauded. Earlier that week, Mark had gotten the workers to build a safety rail around the podium to keep Nigel from swaying too far while he was conducting. As Nigel stepped up on the podium, Mark took his hand and gave him the baton. Nigel was now in position as the conductor, so Maria and Mark left the stage.

Nigel slowly turned towards the audience while holding onto the rail.

"Good evening. Come with me as we travel to a small village deep in Old Mexico. It is early morning and the sun is about to rise. Then slowly, one by one the people come out of their houses and start to decorate the streets, and food vendors prepare themselves on every corner of the plaza. The grass is green, the air is cool, and children run about. Imagine the aura of happiness as they prepare... for fiesta."

Nigel turned around and raised his baton. It was *Huapango*, a famous Mexican piece.

All eyes were on the conductor.

The critics were also in the audience. Nigel was an unknown to them and to most, it probably appeared to be simply a spectacle. They came ready to pounce.

After *Huapango*, there was a standing ovation.

The next day in the entertainment section of the city newspaper, they wrote how profound Nigel's introduction to "Huapango" was and how it seemed to give the audience a visual perspective to accompany the music.

One of our major critics wrote: "Nigel Ledger creates a rare and unique excitement in his manner of conducting, enticing the listener into an almost uncontrollable 'racing of the heart' as they follow his every move, and are transported into an adventure. Maestro Ledger lives in the music."

We all considered the first night to be a success. On the second performance, we had a full house. The word had gotten out and everyone suddenly wanted to see the blind maestro. Ticket sales were up.

One day during a short rehearsal break, Maria escorted Nigel to the piano. As he sat down, he began to tinker with various chords to see how they sounded. When the thirty minutes of break were nearly over, many of the players strolled back inside and walked up to the piano to listen.

Nigel gently settled on Verdi's *Va Pensiero*. Then Maria started to lightly sing along. She had sung this before. What's more, the orchestra also knew

Va Pensiero, as they had played it many times.

Maria told the players standing around her, "Sing with me. Everyone."

Immediately one of the trumpet players and then others tried to confess that they couldn't sing.

Nigel stopped and said with an encouraging tone, "Nonsense! Everyone in orchestras can sing. You were all born with a sense of tone and trained in timing. Everyone sing and let us make a choir. It will be fun."

Shy and giggly, grinning from ear to ear, they sang along with Maria.

After about thirty seconds, Nigel halted.

"Stop. I have an idea," He said. "All of the men stand on the left side of the piano, and the ladies on the right."

The players moved into position and then Nigel began to animate his instructions with his hands.

"This time when you sing, I want you to look into each other's eyes and gesture to them like they are your lovers on the other side of a wide river. Make them believe with your voice and expressions how you long to be with them again."

Then the trumpet player spoke up, "How can we do that? *Va Pensiero* is about Hebrew slaves in bondage."

"Oh! You give me heartburn," Nigel complained. "This is an exercise in passion. Besides, unless you speak Italian, no one knows what the hell you're saying. Now sing."

As Nigel began again, Maria led the way with her fantastic voice and then gestures. Shortly into the piece, the men and women were singing from their hearts, gesturing to each other like lovers separated by a great chasm.

Seeing this, Mark Chastain quietly slipped up on stage and got the attention of the remainder of players already seated.

"*Va Pensiero,*" he said quietly.

Only an accomplished professional could have joined in so quietly and gently as Mark did.

Within seconds, their voices became louder as each player found their confidence. Looking into one another's eyes while acting out their gestures of sorrow, longing, and love had pushed them into an untapped emotional state.

At the end of *Va Pensiero,* many were in tears. Some were laughing, and some embraced each other.

These were once students of some of the best music academies from all over the globe. They were accomplished sight readers and masters of their instruments, yet some of them had forgotten the emotional power that music could have over a person's spirit. Nigel reminded them of that.

It had been six weeks and nearly every performance was sold out. The gamble with Nigel was a success. Now it was time to prepare for the second theme, *Great Classical Composers.* The orchestra had three days to ready themselves before the first concert.

One day during rehearsal, I spotted Reginal sitting in the back of the theater. He was watching Mark conduct. I slipped in one row behind him, walked over, and sat down.

Something was on my mind and I needed to talk to him. I had noticed that Mark had grown distant. He wasn't his usual self. There was an unhappiness in the air.

"Reginal," I asked, "is there something wrong with our resident conductor?"

"Yes," Reginal sadly said. "We have taken his glory and passed it to a blind man. It's like sticking a knife in one's pride. I just hope we can hang on to him."

My face slumped, "That's an alarming statement, Reginal. I thought things were finally coming together. To get upset about such a frivolous thing..."

Reginal turned around and interrupted me, "Hammond! I'm going to tell you something. You are not to repeat it to anyone..."

I could tell by the look on his face, he was very serious. "Not a word. Do you understand?" Reginal reiterated.

"Sure, Reginal. I won't say a word."

Reginal found a more comfortable position, "When Mark Chastain was a young man, he went to Palermo to study music composition under Nigel. That was many years ago, when Nigel still had his sight. Nigel doesn't know or remember Mark."

"Well, I didn't know that." Surprised as I was, I asked, "So is that the big secret?"

"Not quite. Mark was in Italy for only two days when something went terribly wrong. On his second night, he went drinking with some of the other students in a local tavern. There was a fight, and a local man was killed. Mark was tried and convicted in an Italian court. Instead of going to prison, Italy deported him back to the United States. It never made the front pages here in the states, but it was a big deal in Italy."

"Mark told you this?"

"No, he didn't," Reginal continued. "I was in study at Rome, and I could read Italian in the newspapers. I remember the incident very well."

Now I was curious, "Why didn't you tell someone? Why didn't he?"

"To avoid reliving the shame, Hammond. Mark is on his own road to redemption. I believe he's entitled to that."

I was compelled to understand what Reginal was trying to tell me, "And I should be a little understanding? Right?"

"Yes. This is the cross that he alone has had to bear." Then he paused and looked at Mark conducting, "Mark admires Nigel immensely. Anyone can see that, but I also think that Mark is thankful Nigel doesn't remember him."

I just sat there shaking my head, trying to get everything straight. This was going to be a mental burden for me. I was always a man of numbers, not secrets. I was almost sorry Reginal had told me the story, but I was bound to keep his secret.

Great Classic Composers was sold out the first night. Mark Chastain started the night with Copland's "Rodeo." His following four performances were equally impressive. I think he received a louder applause than any of the previous nights. When he turned to bow to the people, I could see the gladness in his face, but it didn't last.

After Mark introduced Nigel, he walked backstage and stood with me. Nigel turned around and addressed the audience.

"Good evening ladies and gentlemen. Imagine with me, as we experience the excitement of an adventure... running and jumping and chasing. The good battling the evil... and finally the victory after battle. Ride with me and Shostakovich as we vanquish the enemy in his *Symphony No. 10*.

Again, it was an attack on the senses that stunned the audience. They seemed unaware that they were sitting on the edge of their seats, listening intensely and imagining the adventure. They marveled at Nigel's conducting and were mesmerized by his dance. The audience roared with applause.

Without turning his head and looking at me, Mark blurted out, "I could be out of a job."

"We'll never let you go, Mark," I tried to reassure him. "You're too important to the symphony."

Mark looked at me with a blank stare, "Don't patronize me, Hammond." Then he walked away.

I should have kept my mouth shut; now I felt terrible. It didn't come out the way I wanted it to, and now Mark was conscious of my lame efforts.

It was now time for the third seasonal theme, *Lesser-Known Film Scores*. The orchestra had two weeks to prepare and Nigel was about to shake things up.

Even before the first rehearsal, there were rumbling complaints from the players. The fear was that they would be playing the hit pieces that everyone had already heard a million times before—simple, elementary, and worn out. They were also concerned with the length of the scores because so many were too short.

Nigel and Mark inevitably caught wind of the rumblings and called for a meeting. The entire orchestra left the stage and moved to the more comfortable seats where the audience sat. This told them that the meeting might run long.

Nigel explained to them that the entire performance would be lesser-known film pieces. Once he named some of the film scores that they didn't recognize, the players were more at ease with the program. That helped.

"Don't harbor false illusions about soundtracks," Nigel told them. "They are still classical pieces. The difference between soundtracks and conventional works are the time constraints. Soundtracks have no other choice but to immediately grab the emotions. That makes it fun for everyone. You deliver twice the power in half the time."

Then Nigel called out Greta Vanderbriet, the orchestra's piano player, "Greta! Are you here?"

Greta shyly stuck up her hand and squeaked, "I'm here."

Greta was our symphony piano player, and the most unusual person I have ever met. She hid behind a pair of thick glasses that could set paper on fire, and yet she was a genius musician that could play anything you put in front of her. However, she had a problem with self-confidence. Especially when she knew she was going to be in the spotlight, as we discovered.

Greta was pushing fifty years and had never been married. In fact, what few friends she had couldn't even recall her ever having a boyfriend.

Nigel had big plans for Greta. He was going to have her play two key pieces while the symphony's cameras were on her and her hands, showing her on the big screen for the audience.

Nigel sent Maria to talk to Greta about her assignment, but Greta turned into a nervous wreck. Greta was comfortable in the background, but the prospect of cameras on her performance gave her anxiety attacks. Maria's assignment turned out to be a counseling session complete with a paper bag for hyperventilating.

Nigel was also going to add a small chorus that Maria would conduct. That was going to be a neat trick, since we didn't have a chorus and certainly didn't have the budget for one. So, the first thing Nigel did was address the orchestra for their help. We recruited husbands, wives, sons, and daughters from the families of the orchestra. As it turned out, everyone was anxious to participate. We acquired eighteen people, but that wasn't enough.

Maria and Reginal went to the local high schools and colleges to infiltrate their music departments. They recruited over forty more volunteers. That provided us with about sixty singers, and then Maria insisted we stop recruiting.

The amazing thing was that we acquired everyone for free. The older ones saw this as a once-in-a-lifetime opportunity, and for the younger ones, it was a way to have some fun.

During rehearsals, our chorus members were the first ones through the doors, bringing vibrant and refreshing attitudes. Their ages ranged anywhere from fourteen to fifty years old. Those were very exciting days.

Opening night for *Lesser-Known Film Scores* produced an unforeseen effect. We had a packed house. Our blind maestro had set the precedent and everyone in San Antonio was expecting more of the same.

This time Mark would conduct the first half of the program and Nigel would conduct the second half.

Mark came on stage and bowed to the audience. Without saying a word, he took to the podium and raised his arms. Then he began. It was the theme from *The 13th Warrior: Sound of the Northmen*. Very powerful. Very moving.

Mark went on to conduct *Storm*, from *Elizabeth the Golden Age*, written by Craig Armstrong. Then it was *Whisper of a Thrill* from *Meet Joe Black*, written by James Horner.

On the final piece, he conducted *Crusaders*, from *Kingdom of Heaven*. The chorus had a major part, and they sounded fantastic.

After the intermission, Maria led Nigel to the podium and he started with *Over the Moon*, from the movie *E.T. the Extra-Terrestrial*. This piece was made for the piano and Greta was in the spotlight.

I never realized how complicated it was until I watched her on the big screen above the orchestra. I was impressed and proud of her at the same time. The music was absolutely beautiful.

Before the second piece, Nigel told the audience a short tale of King Arthur and related it to the movie, *First Knight*.

"It was the legend of King Arthur and the love he had for his country and Queen Guinevere that set the stage for the betrayal by Sir Lancelot. In the end, King Arthur's life is taken by Meleagant's army, a rival of the King. You are about to hear the music to King Arthur's funeral as he is buried at sea, *Camelot Lives*."

The stage was thus set. This was his psychological approach to captivate his audience during an emotional piece. Nigel had the unique talent to make the audience believe they were actually there in the scene of the movie.

The remainder of the night, he conducted pieces from great composers like Jerry Goldsmith, John Williams, and a finale of a three-movement, special arrangement of Thomas Newman's *Road to Perdition, Splice*.

It seemed like our three-hour program went fast. At the end of the night the audience gave Nigel a standing ovation.

Ticket sales were finally above normal. We were packed at over seventy-five percent capacity for the remainder of the season. The board members were happy and Reginal was finally able to relax.

The Alamo City Orchestra was now known abroad for having something that no one else had, a blind phenom. What the public didn't know was that Nigel Ledger was not scheduled to return the following season.

One day during a post-season rehearsal, Mark Chastain had finished a session with the orchestra when he decided he needed some time alone. Everyone could see his spirits were down. He walked into what he thought was the empty conference room, closed the door, and slowly walked over to the widow. There, he stood for a moment in silence and stared at the people out on the street.

"Some conductor you are," he said aloud, then put both hands in his pockets and slumped his shoulders. Obviously depressed, as if his career was finished, "What now?" he concluded.

Mark was so focused on the window he didn't see Nigel sitting at the dark end of the conference room, but Nigel had heard every word.

"Make them cry," Nigel announced from the darkness.

Startled by Nigel's presence, Mark quickly turned around. "Nigel? How'd you slip in here?"

"I had Maria bring me. Sometimes the excitement is overwhelming. Silence can have its own healing qualities."

Mark slowly walked over to one of the chairs and sat down. "I've got to hand it to you, Nigel. You command the audience...and make them beckon... Makes me want to gouge out my own eyes."

There were ten seconds of silence as Nigel was thinking what to say. Then he gently took his cane off of his lap and placed the end of it on the floor. "Of all the students I have taught, you had the most superior and dynamic passion for music I have ever seen. Your presence has always been inspiring."

Mark's eyes suddenly opened wide. He slowly cocked his head to look at Nigel. "I beg your pardon?"

"You think I didn't remember you? I might not be able to see, but I am far from blind. I've been watching you for years. Following you. I remember."

His secret and identity discovered, Mark lowered his head and expelled a held breath of air. "All this time... well... Nigel. I guess you also remember that in Italy, I'm still a murderer."

Nigel was quick to answer, "Unfortunate events. And that is what haunts you so many years after. You have not forgiven yourself for it, Mark. Since Italy you have walked a self-imposed line of punishment...obeying all of the rules...too many rules. It is time for you to forgive yourself. It's time for you to release your passions again."

Mark just shook his head, "Funny. I vaguely remember what that felt like. But I don't think I can get it back anymore, Nigel."

Nigel stood up from his chair, put his cane in front of him and felt his way up to Mark. "Stand up for me. Please," he asked Mark.

Mark stood up. Nigel walked in close and placed his left hand on his shoulder. Then he hooked his cane over his arm and reached out with his right hand, "Let me see you again," he asked ever so gently.

Nigel slowly ran his fingers down Mark's face, then placed his hand on Mark's other shoulder.

"Your talent is the passion. One that has it, never loses it. You must flourish and thrive again. My faithful, young, and promising student. You are not a conductor of a band. You are...Mark Chastain, maestro of a symphony."

As the father that loved his son, this was Nigel's attempt to help Mark vanquish his inner demons, that he would never live in perpetuity again.

That time of the year had come around again. Nigel was due his annual eye exam. And as usual, after the exam, he would take Maria on their annual stroll along the San Antonio Riverwalk. It was always cooler that time of year and there were fewer tourist to contend with.

In the small foyer of Maria's residence, Nigel stood waiting for Maria to bring him his coat. She helped him put it on and then straightened his bow-tie with a personal touch.

"Who knows, Nigel. The eye doctors have made many advances over the years. Maybe they can relieve your headaches...at least."

"Yes perhaps, my dear. But I never get my hopes up too much. I've grown rather accustomed to my disability. However! If I had but only one wish, it would be to see your beautiful face again. Just once so I could hold you in awe." Nigel told her.

Maria smiled at him in admiration as she pulled his coat together for him and buttoned the front. "I am no longer a young woman, Nigel. I am old and no longer beautiful."

"Preposterous!" Nigel declared, "I know beauty when I see it. I know beauty when I smell it. And most of all...I know it is real when it flutters my heart. You... flutter my heart," Nigel stood up straight and tall, "Now. How do I look?"

"Very handsome. Like Wagner incarnate."

"Great," Nigel said with a sarcastic voice. "He's been dead for a hundred years. Now let's go before I am."

Maria reached up and gave Nigel a short kiss on the lips. "My inspiration." She opened the door and they were gone.

I felt like Reginal's idea was out of line. He wanted to sign Nigel for another season while Nigel was still hot and riding on the wave of euphoria. I can't say I blamed him, but this was exactly what Nigel didn't want. My concern was that we might be pushing Nigel a little bit too much. After all, he was already an old man when we started. But Reginal was the director, and he wanted him for at least one more season. So did the board members.

After two months into the off-season, Reginal finally worked up the courage and a plan. Reginal and Mark would make a proposal to sign Nigel for one additional season. Everyone knew beforehand that this was a delicate matter, convincing Nigel to return. Every time we discussed our approach, I noticed everyone holding their breath and keeping their fingers crossed.

Finally on a bright sunny day, Reginal had me phone Maria's house and make quick arrangements for us to come over later that afternoon.

Maria lived in an old section of San Antonio where the houses were styled between Victorian and Old Plantation. The streets were encompassed by giant oaks and pecan trees, towering and protecting this old-money neighborhood for the last hundred years.

Maria's house had four small, white columns holding an extended porch that jutted out onto the brick driveway. Her lawn was just as elegant as she was in person.

All three of us walked to the door and I knocked.

When she opened the door, she was obviously apprehensive about our visit. Nevertheless, she invited us in and we all sat down in her living room.

"Maria," Reginal began, "we would like to talk to Nigel and you about another season. Is Nigel about somewhere?"

Maria never smiled. She just looked at him as we all felt an uncomfortable silence came over the room. Seconds went by. Everyone could sense something was not right.

"Maria?" Reginal inquired again. "Is Nigel alright?"

Maria nodded her head, "Yes. Yes, he's fine... but he's not here. He went back to Palermo."

"Palermo," Mark softly uttered as he stared at the floor.

"Palermo? Does he have family there?" Reginal asked.

Maria shook her head, "No. He went there to compose."

"To compose?" Reginal blurted as if he couldn't believe it.

"Gentlemen. I need to tell you of recent events," Maria began. "I took him to the doctor for his annual eye exam about a month ago and the doctors restored his sight, almost perfectly."

We just stared at her with our jaws hanging.

"Oh my god. That's like... a miracle," I sputtered.

Maria continued, "Yes. Nigel was so excited. I took him to all the sights of the city. For him, it was like seeing everything for the first time again."

"That is amazing! We could have celebrated with him," Reginal added.

"There's more to his blessing," Maria continued. "He discovered he could no longer conduct. His restored vision made him too self-aware, too self-conscience of his own movements to wield the movements that took him so long to develop, no matter how hard he tried. I tried to help him, but it was no longer there."

There was a long pause as we all looked at each other, not knowing what to say or do.

Reginal leaned back on the couch and rubbed his hands over his thighs a few times. "Well. That's good for Nigel. Of course, that's not so good for the orchestra. I'm sure we can come up with some kind of gimmick or something."

Answering Reginal's concern, "Nigel wanted me to tell everyone… just one departing bit of advice."

"What was that?" Reginal asked.

"Everything you need for success," with a straight face, she looked at Mark, "you already have."

"I don't think I understand. Can you be more specific?" Reginal probed.

Maria quickly looked at me and changed the subject, "Hammond! Have you talked to Greta Vanderbriet?"

"What?" I said. "Greta? No. Did I screw up her pay?"

"Talk to her, Hammond." Maria insisted.

The visit was a good news, bad news encounter. We went back to our offices and resumed life. Reginal put together another season of performances and I, Hammond the bookkeeper, watched the numbers.

From time to time, Maria would drop by to see everyone and give us some updates. Evidently Nigel wanted to finish a composition he was working on when he lost his sight, thirty years before. And he wanted to finish it while he still had his faculties. He was also teaching again in Palermo.

The atmosphere wasn't the same without Nigel and Maria. We had lost our beloved piano tuner, the only one we ever knew, as well as an inspirational teacher.

However, the machine kept turning. The collective made subtle changes to the organization, seemingly unconcerned with detail or impartial with ranking. A better lighting system, a new tuning device for the piano, things that most didn't have an opinion on. It was like no one really cared. Most of all, time dragged on monotonously for everyone. Boring days of rehearsal accompanied with the poor lighting of drab colors seemed to plague the air we were breathing. Nothing was the same. We all missed Nigel.

On the last day of rehearsal before opening night, Maria came by and caught Mark in his office. She closed the door behind her, stood there, and looked at him through watery eyes.

Never taking his gaze off of her, he stood up from his desk and walked over to her. "Maria? What's happened?"

"Nigel is gone. He had a massive stroke."

"Dead?" Mark asked.

Maria nodded, "Yes."

They shared a solemn moment of grief with each other and held onto each other to weep.

Then Maria pulled away, placed her hands lovingly around Mark's face, and did her best to talk through the tears. "When Nigel retired, he only wanted to do one thing—come to San Antonio and see you develop. We have both been watching and following you for years... from a distance. He said you reminded him of himself when he was young. Honor Nigel, Mark. Take his place."

"How?" Mark asked.

"Don't concern yourself with perfection. Conduct with your heart, and make them cry."

The news of Nigel's death had a devastating impact on all of the musicians. Rehearsal was cancelled. The next time they would meet would be in two days, opening night.

That night a cold front blew in and dropped the temperature at least thirty degrees. The streets downtown looked largely abandoned. No special events were happening anyway. No sports events. No large conventions to speak of, just the cold air blowing in from the north.

It made people bundle themselves to stay warm. Everyone's pace began to quicken and people became more inquisitive with one another on a personal basis. I could see people's spirits being slowly lifted. Whether it was just a simple change of weather, or the continuation of tears that washed away our sadness wasn't important. The fact was that the orchestra had turned the corner and was on the road to recovery.

I don't know exactly how it happened, but I took Greta on a date. She never stopped talking the entire night. I had a great time and look forward to our next date.

Opening night the entire orchestra strolled in and took their seats. Mark Chastain walked out on stage and up onto the podium. As was customary, the audience applauded the conductor and then an unexpected silence overcame the music hall.

Mark faced the orchestra and stood there with his hands folded in front. He looked down at the music stand to orientate himself with the sheet music, then dismissed the action and slowly looked up at his orchestra. All of the players were looking back at him intensely. It was a look of sadness. There were also the stares of concern. Concern for the well-being of their conductor.

Then Mark spoke in a low tone so only they could hear, "For our piano tuner, Nigel Ledger."

There were smiles of solidarity. Then the conductor raised his baton and the orchestra plunged into Rimsky-Korsakov's *Fandango Asturiano*.

Immediately, everyone could see Mark had changed his style of conducting, for every sweep of his baton was now more pronounced. Periodically closing his eyes, he would transport himself into the composer's mind, as if he were standing with Korsakov himself on the bow of a ship during a terrible storm. Mark had made this personal.

At the end of the piece, the audience applauded. Then slowly, one by one they stood until it became a standing ovation.

Reginal, Maria, and myself were there. So were the critics. They wrote:

> *Mark Chastain creates a rare and unique excitement*
> *in his manner of conducting, enticing the listener into an almost*
> *uncontrollable 'racing of the heart' as they follow his every move*
> *and are transported into an adventure. Maestro Chastain lives*
> *in the music.*

35

Good Deeds

I LOVE MY TWO older brothers. When we were growing up, they took me everywhere they went. We went down every street, along miles of sandy beach, and to almost all the high school games. That was itself, a big chore. When I was seven I came down with a bad fever that left me paralyzed. Mama said I was lucky the fever didn't take all of me. My body might have left me with a disability, but my advantage was that I had a brain as big as a watermelon.

I went straight to a wheelchair. Later on I graduated to leg braces and then on a good day, a walking cane.

Most of the time I went with my brothers, but since I had half their strength, I was the slowest and always the last one out the door.

Despite my problems, I was one of the luckiest kids in Galveston. Every summer day when our chores were done we had a daily routine. My brothers would roll my chair out the front door, hook it to one of their bicycles and off we would go down the streets. We learned the hard way that my wheelchair couldn't steer or stop. Of course, that was after some spectacular crashes. I ended up in the ditch most of the time, but nobody got hurt. Not really.

Later on my brothers added three bicycle wheels and a handbrake to my wheelchair. That did the job and earned me the name, "Roller Boy."

I may have been crippled, but it didn't matter to my brothers. I was the smart one of the three and they needed me to keep them out of trouble. That was a full-time job.

My brothers always meant well. They made do with what they had by taking shortcuts. That was the way they did things, always shortcuts. Two black kids that were always looking for something new and exciting to break the monotony of a summer day, but to outsiders, I suppose they gave the impression that they were a long train of trouble. The truth is that they didn't have a dishonest bone in their bodies. They just weren't that smart when it came to certain things. Shortcuts kept them constantly running from trouble and under the watchful eyes of Mama and Uncle Bud.

When it came to having fun, they never left me out. Like the time Rock found a bunch of rubber bicycle tubes and made a human slingshot down at one of the fishing piers. All it took was tying the two ends to the last post at the end of the pier and a bunch of manpower to load it. It took six people to pull back the middle and tie it off with a bad piece of old rope. Sometimes it would be so tight it sounded like a guitar string. It was a regular mechanical marvel.

Once a person was in the middle of the slingshot and ready to be launched, someone would cut the rope and catapult your ass up in the air and across the water.

When it was my turn to go, they strapped me down in my wheelchair and tied a lifejacket around my waist. As soon as that rope was cut, I took off at warp speed; one of the front wheels hit the last post on the pier, spinning me like an out-of-control top. The whole world was going around until I hit the water, my lifejacket popped off, and I sunk to the bottom. Just for a second I had a chance to open my eyes and marvel at my new surroundings. Before I could get scared, here came Rock and Runner to my rescue, pulling me out the water with seaweed hanging off my head. It was a lot of fun.

For my sixteenth birthday, Rock and Runner found an old dune buggy and somehow got the motor running. It had lights and enough room for me to carry my wheelchair and a stick, which I used as a walking cane from time to time. It was the perfect setup. I could get around with no help from anybody. That's the way I liked it. That is, except for one night when I rounded a corner and hit a giant alligator that was in the middle of the street. My dune buggy never made it all the way. It stopped right in the middle of its back, high-centered.

He must have weighed nine-hundred pounds and was three feet thick at the middle. I wasn't going nowhere. I was right on top of the biggest damn alligator Galveston could offer, and he was mad. He'd open up that big mouth of his and hiss and groan at me, so I grabbed my stick and whopped him on the nose every time I thought he needed calming down.

Luckily for me, Rock and Runner had their cell phones and were close by. When they came sliding around the corner, they stopped with their head-lights on the accident. I was sure glad to see them.

"I ain't believing my eyes," Runner said.

I yelled back, "Get me out of here!"

"Roller Boy, you best stay still," Rock added. "You fall out one side and he'll eat you... and you fall out the other side and he'll whop you with his tail. That's one pissed off lizard."

The alligator opened his mouth and snarled at me, so I whacked him with my stick again. "From up here he looks more like a dinosaur! I been fight-ing him off for the last fifteen minutes. Ya'll need to do something."

Then here came the 'Po Po,' or the police. It was Officer Ray from the Galveston Police Department. Everybody knew Ray.

Officer Ray was just as amazed at the situation as we were, so he did what the policemen did on TV, he called someone with a camera and a profes-sional at gossip—the local newspaper.

They took pictures of me in the dune buggy, on top of that alligator. They managed to get me out of the dune buggy from the front. Then they threw a chain on the front and pulled it slowly over the alligators back. It must have hurt that old alligator, because before it went too far, the alligator turned around and grabbed the back tire, ripping it right off the rim. Then, true to form and reputation, the reptile slid off into the ditch with the tire still in its mouth.

Officer Ray looked at me, trying not to laugh, "If you want your tire back, you'll have to get it yourself. My advice is to let him have it. Maybe it'll clog him up enough for him to stop eating all the ducks at the golf course."

The plan was to not tell Mama what happened until the next morning at the end of breakfast. Mama had the tendency to throw a high-ball fit every time she heard about one of our close-call adventures. We were going to ease her into the story, slowly.

The next morning started out smooth and peaceful. So much so that we found ourselves looking at each other, wondering who was going to break the news. If we could have got away with it, we probably wouldn't have uttered a word.

Then, as luck would have it, there was a knock on the door. When Mama walked over to answer it, Rock and Runner stared at each other and I could see the concern in their eyes. The shit was about to hit the fan.

Within seconds, Mama yelled, "Rock, you and Runner get your black asses in here!"

It was Officer Ray again. When Rock and Runner walked up to the door. He held up a piece of paper, "Ya'll know that dune buggy that was parked on the alligator? It was stolen. Did you know that?"

Rock tried to explain, "We found it in a junk yard."

Mama turned around and hit Rock on the head with her wooden spoon. It went flying in two pieces.

That's why he was called Rock. Years ago, when Daddy was still alive, he slapped Rock on the head and busted a blood vessel in his hand. He was always known to have a head as hard as a rock.

Runner didn't wait around for the second spoon to be broken, he took off out the back door and disappeared into the brush. He wasn't running from Officer Ray. He was running from Mama.

That's how Runner got his name. Daddy, rest his soul, was going to "whip his ass" one day as he put it, but my brother took off before he could get his belt. That's why we always called him Runner.

"Ain't you going to chase him?" asked Mama.

Officer Ray handed her the morning paper. "Nah. He runs too fast. Besides, I don't think he's running from me. Just tell your boys to see the judge on Wednesday morning. He'll probably work something out. He's a good judge."

I never knew the ownership of the dune buggy was in question. My absent-minded brothers evidently didn't either. It's not like they stole it right off the street, it was in an old junk yard getting ready for scrap. And that was the constant problem. My brothers were part-time idiots. This kind of thing was always happening with them as a result of their shortcuts. It seems like all their lives they took the ideas that only a frog could think of, and turned them into big problems. Never enough for serious trouble, but stupid things like taking an old dune buggy from someone we all knew would have given it to them for free if they had asked.

There was also the time they took two bald tires from behind a service station without permission, and another when they used an old lady's purse found on the pier to carry stinky bait shrimp. Who steals bald tires? What's more, who's got the guts to be caught carrying shrimp in a woman's pink purse? When Officer Ray left, Mama walked back into the kitchen where I was still sitting at the table. She looked mad. That is, until I watched her eyes widen as she finally looked at the front page of the newspaper Officer Ray gave her. Then I honestly thought she was going to faint.

"Roller Boy? I know there's got to be a story behind this. Please make it good?" Then she dropped the paper on the table and sit down in the chair. "This is the reason I got grey hair. I should have had girls."

There I was on the front page of the Galveston paper, a picture of me standing in my dune buggy, looking at the camera through my thick glasses, and that big old alligator underneath me with his mouth wide open.

All I could do was make a proud declaration, "I'm famous." Mama just placed her hands over her face and groaned.

After the judge found that the dune buggy was actually abandoned in a dump, a deal was made with the county attorney to defer all charges. They called it deferred adjudication. In the meantime, they were to do community service and stay out of trouble for six months.

Mama tried to get the judge to put them in jail. She told the judge that a little incarceration and jail food might do them some good, but the judge didn't go for it. He insisted on community service, which was going to be riding the ferry every day over to the adjacent island and picking up trash along

Bolivar Peninsula beach.

After court, with their heads hanging low from a minutiae of shame, Runner and Rock decided they wanted to go down to the shrimp docks and see our Uncle Bud. Our Uncle Bud had been a shrimper for as long as there had been shrimp in the ocean. At seventy years old, he was an expert at catching shrimp, but yet as cantankerous as that old alligator.

I went with them because Mama had that bad look again. She always felt a little better when I was with them. They were always less likely to get in trouble when someone with a brain was around, even if I was in a wheelchair.

Rock and Runner walked down the dock and jumped aboard Uncle Bud's shrimp boat. They looked around, but Uncle Bud was not there, so they grabbed a few things from the boat and we left. Uncle Bud was waiting for us when we came out of the head of the dock, standing there in his white boots and wrinkly face.

"Did I give you permission to go on my boat?" Uncle Bud asked.

"You weren't there, Uncle Bud." Rock tried to explain.

"We just needed to borrow a few things..." Runner continued.

"You don't take liberties without permission. How many times I got to tell you that? You know what I mean by liberties, Runner? You know what that is?" pressuring them more.

"It's a statue in New York?" Runner answered.

"No, dammit!" Bud scolded them, "You boys ain't got the sense of mullet. I swear."

Bud might have been old, but he was sharp.

Uncle Bud saw a candy bar in Runner's pocket, so he snatched it. "What the hell? You found this in my wheelhouse, didn't you? I was saving this for later."

Rock said, "I didn't take any of your food, Uncle Bud."

Uncle Bud caught the glimpse of plier handles sticking out of his back pocket. "Give me that."

Rock surrendered the pliers reluctantly.

"You little thieving bastards. Every time you come around my boat, something comes up missing." He scolded them further, "Don't you know a man's got to ask before he takes?"

Runner held up the safety vest. "Uncle Bud, can we borrow this?"

"Of course you can. See how easy that was? Now get your asses out of here. Go do your sentences."

We rolled past Uncle Bud and my brothers' heads were hanging low.

Before we got too far, he yelled at everybody again. "Hey! After you boys get finished with the beach, ya'll come back and we'll rebuild some boat motors... make some real money." He turned his back, but we could still hear him say, "Damn mullet heads." That gave something for Rock and Runner to look forward to.

I never met one, but I think Uncle Bud could have made a good pirate. After all he was mean as hell when he wanted to be. All he needed was a parrot on his shoulder and a patch over one eye.

Uncle Bud taught Rock and Runner all he could about engines, but because of their youth and his lack of patience, the lessons were always cut short. What Rock and Runner did know about engines was because of Uncle Bud and they used it to their advantage.

Before we got back to the house, we stopped at a construction site and watched a big bulldozer pushing dirt. The job site had heavy equipment running back and forth, pushing, piling, and loading the dirt onto dump trucks. The backup alarms, roaring diesels, and smell of exhaust made everyone envious to be there.

"I can drive that," Rock said.

"You ain't even been in one of those things before," Runner replied.

"It don't matter. All it is, is controls hooked up to cables and hydraulics, powered by a motor. Simple," Rock continued.

The foreman of the job was a huge white man, wearing a white shirt and a blue hard hat. He kept looking over at us. It was like we were intruding on his property or something and it made us nervous.

"That man must to be the boss," I said. "Think he would hire us... you know... give us a real job?"

Runner exhaled a big breath. It was as if he knew the answer without saying. "What do you think he sees when he looks at us?"

"That we probably stole something. No one he wants to hire us, that's for sure," Rock said.

"Yeah. He don't even like us watching," Runner said.

The foreman watched us closely. There had been thefts on his job site during the past. There was nothing to say he wasn't looking at three mischievous thieves at that very moment.

Runner was right. We didn't look like construction workers. We looked like up-to-no-good beach bums, not dressed in the best of clothes, two street kids pushing their little brother around in wheelchair. We didn't look the part.

Rock stood up and put his hands in his pockets. "We graduate high school this year and we need jobs."

Runner brought up an idea that was considered taboo in our family.

"Sell dope to the tourists down on the beach? That's where the money is."

I spoke up loudly, "Mama don't allow no dope. You know that," hoping I got his attention.

Runner just looked at me and sighed. "Yeah... I know." The look on his face told me he knew I was right. "Let's get out of here."

It was the first time all three of us brothers were forced to look into our futures. The outcome was not promising.

We weren't high class, but we weren't low class either. We were born into circumstances where we had to work for anything we were to get. We were black middle-class kids that knew we needed jobs, but had no idea where to start.

Two days passed and it was time for Rock and Runner to do their community service; they grabbed their safety vests and reported to the county yard where a bus took everyone across the Bolivar Cut on the ferry. There was a full busload of men to accompany them, also working off their community debts.

The plan was to work a half day cleaning the Bolivar beach of trash. Normally they would have worked all day, but there was a storm brewing in the Gulf of Mexico, and they were already calling it Hurricane *Ike*.

Picking up trash on the beach was a useless task. Everyone knew that a hurricane would make a bigger mess than even an army of men could pick up. And to cleanup before the storm was absolutely ridiculous. They were just there to work off their community service.

The bus passed Crystal Beach then went twenty miles farther, and dropped off the first two men. Those first two were Rock and Runner.

With their plastic garbage bags in hand, Rock and Runner started walking back towards Point Bolivar along the beach, picking up trash. At the end of three hours they had left a long trail of trash bags along the beach road and never saw another person. What they did notice was the ocean turning green at the third sand-bar where the first waves were breaking. The winds were steadily picking up and the clouds to the east were turning dark. They were heavy with rain. It was only a matter of time; Hurricane *Ike* was coming a little sooner than later and the giant blue swells they were seeing would likely cover everything on the beach.

There were no alarming thoughts to Rock and Runner. Surviving a hurricane on the Gulf Coast was considered routine. Although there was that one that hit in 1900, when one of the biggest hurricanes killed 8,000 people on Galveston Island. It was called *Carla*. Locals know about hurricanes and now with modern communications and weather satellites, they're taken in stride.

Sometime during the cleanup, Rock and Runner noticed a small shrimp boat heading straight for shore as fast as it could go. That was rather unusual.

"Look at that fool," Rock said.

The longer they watched, the more they concluded there was a problem.

Runner put down his bag, "Something is wrong."

The shrimp boat went right over the third sand bar, never slowing down. By the time it hit the second sand bar, the engine stalled, making the boat drift sideways. The next wave rolled the boat over on its side and it was instantly swamped. Then there were cries from within the boat, "Help!"

Rock dropped his plastic bag full of trash, "They're in trouble, Runner!"

"Let's go!" Runner shouted.

Without thinking, Runner and Rock jumped into the surf like life-guards. When they reached the boat, they were greeted by a scared twelve-year-old boy. His father, the captain, was having a heart attack, but before he ran aground, he had managed to call 9-1-1.

With great effort, Rock and Runner managed to pull both out of the boat and drag them back to shore and then up to the highway.

Running with their emergency lights and no sirens, an ambulance pulled up from the north and stopped. Three EMTs jumped out with a stretcher. Within seconds they had the victim and the boy loaded in the ambulance.

The wind and crashing waves were too loud for normal conversation, so the EMT driver shouted, "We can't take you with us. Hurricane *Ike* is coming early and this place is going to be underwater soon. You guys need to get back to Crystal Beach if you can! You think you can do that?"

Completely soaked and now knowing they would have to abandon their trash pickup, Rock looked at him, "Yes, sir. I think we can."

The EMT driver took a second to look at the boat in the surf and then back at Rock and Runner, "That was a hell of a rescue. Y'all did good."

The EMTs closed the back door and they were gone in a flash.

"It's time for us to get out of here," Rock said.

Runner agreed, "Yeah! We need to get to that bus."

What Rock and Runner didn't know was that the pickup bus had come early and couldn't find them. Nobody ever figured out whether the bus driver ever drove far enough to find them or if Rock and Runner had walked too far north bagging the trash. All the driver knew was what the sheriff radioed to the bus to pick up all the county trash workers early and get them back to the Galveston side. Then for safety's sake, the sheriff gave the evacuation order for all to leave Crystal Beach and Port Bolivar. As soon as the ferries got the last load of people and vehicles, the ferries left the ferry docks and high-tailed it toward the inland docks.

It took several hours for Rock and Runner to walk back to Crystal Beach; all the time they were watching traffic only driving north bound for Beaumont. No one was going south towards Port Bolivar. When they finally got to Crystal Beach, it was abandoned. Not a soul in sight.

Mama and I got to the sheriff's office to pick up Rock and Runner just to find out they had missed the bus. That's when a whole new chapter of family chaos began.

The bus driver, who was a deputy, thought that they had "cut and run" from their duties, and if true, would most likely have to see the judge again.

Mama and I tried to tell him different, but he wouldn't hear it. There was only one thing left for us to do before we went home and weathered the storm, and that was to try to find Officer Ray. Officer Ray was at the police station preparing for the storm.

Mama was so upset she couldn't hardly talk to Officer Ray. I had to do most of the talking.

"Cut and run?" He said in disbelief. "I don't believe it. Not on a day like today." Then he looked Mama straight in the eyes. "Go back home and stay by the phone. I'll do what I can."

Officer Ray knew one thing, but he was careful not to say too much—Rock and Runner weren't on the last ferry. That meant they were stuck at Bolivar or Crystal Beach somewhere by themselves. But Ray was up to his ears in things to do, and the welfare of Rock and Runner were now one of many.

We went back to an empty house and the atmosphere was not good. Mama prayed.

The sky was starting to darken, the winds were wild and most telling, dark green water was showing at the first sandbar. These were all the signs that the hurricane was pushing water from the deep of the Gulf towards the mainland. Hurricane *Ike* was almost here.

Since Rock and Runner were left in such an impossible situation, they did the only thing they could think of: they broke into the sturdiest small beach cabin and prepared to ride out the storm. It was the only structure that was built on heavy pipe stilts and corrugated iron siding, standing twenty feet off the ground. If anything could, this house could protect them from the storm surge. My brothers never did admit, until much later, how scared they were during that storm. They hunkered down and rode out the first assault of the storm. When the eye crossed over and the winds stopped, they reinforced their position, knowing as natives of Galveston that the big winds of the hurricane were about to hit again, this time from the opposite direction.

They never got much sleep that night. The winds howled and wailed making the structure rock back and forth like a shrimp boat in the middle of the ocean. At times they thought the surge would take the structure they were in, but it never did.

Early the next morning when it was all over, both walked out from that elevated cabin unharmed. Their ears were ringing and they were a bit cold, but they had survived. In fact, the only house that was left standing was that metal cabin they took shelter in.

As both of them walked down to the ground level, both were speechless as they looked at the devastation. Concrete foundations seemed to be the only things left, but even some of those were ripped from the ground. The trees and houses were gone, pushed into giant debris piles that were scattered about. The small helipad was only a block away across a cleared field from the cabin they stayed in, but no pilot was going to land there. It was covered with debris too.

Probably what stuck out the most were the roads. They were torn up and blocked by a series of twenty-foot piles of debris, making it impossible to drive.

All Rock and Runner did for the first thirty minutes was walk around with their jaws hanging like refugee survivors of a carpet bombing. The child-like desires of play had left them, only to be replaced by the seriousness at hand. Mother Nature had left a wake of destruction.

All the roads and passes to the north were out. The boat docks at Bolivar were gone. The ferries were gone and their only helipad was covered with crap. Any kind of rescue was going to be difficult.

Suddenly from one of the debris piles a weak voice yelled out, "Help me!"

Rock and Runner looked up to see a seventy-year-old man, all in tatters, slowly crawling his way out of the debris.

My brothers helped the old man out, sat him down, and tried to comfort him, but he was in a frantic state. He told them that he was with five others that tried to ride out the storm. To make matters worse, they were all of the senior citizen class. Their house had blown apart during the night and all of them had weathered the storm in the debris.

Immediately, Rock and Runner went to the pile and began to get the others out. It was a slow and delicate process. One by one they gently helped these seniors out and up onto flat dry ground. Their clothes were torn to shreds, they were weak, dehydrated, and they had every imaginable array of old-person diseases and ailments you could imagine. They were desperate for water and medical attention. My brothers were suddenly overwhelmed with the weight of an unwanted responsibility.

Runner looked at Rock after the last person was out of the debris and sitting on the ground. "What are we going to do now? We ain't got nothing to work with, and Mama probably thinks we're dead."

Rock quickly said, "We can't go anywhere and you know it. The bridges are completely gone, the ferries are a hundred miles away... even the helipad is covered with debris."

Rock was right. Crystal Beach was a mess. There was no telling when anyone would try to rescue them. After all, Galveston had its own set of problems.

Rock asked Runner, "What would Mama do?"

Runner looked around, " 'Take care of business.' That's what she would say. 'Clean up. Help those old folks.' "

"That sounds like something Dad would say... or Uncle Buck," Rock said. "One thing is for sure, if we don't do something good, Mama will have our asses."

Runner agreed, "You got that right. We need to think... what to do next."

Rock and Runner were not accustomed to this kind of emergency situation. They were still in high school, but they knew things, like how to scavenge and build. Those skills they learned from our father and Uncle Bud. There was only one more thing they needed, and that was the fortitude to do the right thing.

Rock and Runner took all of the seniors, one by one, up the stairs of the cabin that they had spent the night in and tended to their needs. They were cold and shivering, hungry and scraped up from their ordeal. They survived the storm by desperately clinging to the debris of what used to be their brick house. After the house fell they rode the storm out in the rain and howling wind. The entire night they clung to each other in the darkness and waited for the eye of the storm to pass. Any other time these people could have recovered quickly and helped themselves, but the storm had zapped all their strength and energy until they were completely helpless, barely able to walk.

Rock found a first aid kit in the cabin and tended to the people that had scrapes and cuts, while Runner managed to feed everyone with a variety of canned goods heated on a propane stove. After he finished there was only one small bottle of propane left. It wasn't great, but the old people appreciated what the boys were doing for them.

My brothers managed to find most of what they needed in that cabin, including fresh bottled water, blankets, and some food. What they couldn't find, they managed to scavenge out of the drift piles and take back to the cabin. It wasn't long until all the seniors were sleeping on the pallets Rock and Runner had laid down. They had been awake all night long.

Once the last one was asleep, the boys walked out on what was left of the balcony and looked over the devastation again. Crystal City was gone.

From their vantage point they could see something dull yellow in one of the piles of debris. It was a bulldozer and a backhoe. The backhoe had been pushed into a debris pile and was nearly on its side.

There wasn't a soul on the island and my brothers didn't have any idea when they would be rescued, so they talked over their plan.

Mama spent the whole night praying. So did I. The next day phones were working, but we couldn't get ahold of Officer Ray. He was right in the middle of rescue operations. We had no idea what *Ike* had done to Crystal Beach. Cleanup had already begun all over the county. The cleanup crews had started from the inside and worked themselves outwards. Hurricane *Ike* had come and gone, leaving a big mess.

The keys to the backhoe and bulldozer were still in the ignitions, probably left behind by construction workers. Rock and Runner pulled the debris off of the machines and checked the oil to make sure they didn't get water inside the engines. They were lucky, because the engines and fuel tanks were full of fuel and oil and didn't appear to have any water inside at all. Then they took the air filters apart and slung the water out of them. Rock found a can of ether in the bulldozer's compartment and Runner managed to find a grease gun on the backhoe. They had everything they needed.

Runner grabbed Rock by the arm just before he climbed aboard the bulldozer, "You know we could get in major trouble for this?"

"Yeah, I know. We're already in trouble, Runner. Might as well clean the place before we go to jail. That's the way I see it."

"I just wanted to make sure we were on the same page," then released his arm.

Rock hopped in the seat of the bulldozer and turned on the ignition, "Besides, I've always wanted to run one of these things. Now give me a shot of ether and let's turn this baby over."

Runner gave the intake a long shot of ether then stepped back. "Try it now!"

Rock turned the key and the engine turned over, but didn't start after five seconds.

"Try it again," hollered Rock.

Runner gave the dozer another squirt, "Hold it about ten seconds."

When the engine turned over it spit thick white smoke out the stack for the first few seconds and then fired right up. The bulldozer coughed, but cleared itself of whatever was in the intake and started to run smoothly.

Runner smiled and yelled at Rock, "I wish Uncle Bud could see us now!"

After they got the bulldozer running, they started the backhoe with no problem.

Nobody told them to, but my brothers decided to put those machines to work. The first thing they did was clear the helipad so that any helicopters could land. Next, they began to clear all the roads from the helipad outward. From that inside location, they cleared all the streets and roads they could get to. The only place they couldn't go was north out of the town. The bridge on highway eighty-seven was gone. No one was going to rescue them from the north. They were completely surrounded by water.

As the day went on, Rock and Runner managed to find two plastic hard hats, so they put them on. Now they looked like regular construction workers.

At the end of the day, about an hour till dark, a Coast Guard helicopter flew over their location. As soon as the pilot saw the large "H" on the helipad, he landed. Rock and Runner both got off their machines and ran out to meet them.

My brothers had mixed feelings about help finally coming. Sure, it was good to see someone coming to the rescue, but Rock and Runner knew they would have to eventually face the music for the liberties they had taken. That was something Uncle Bud had warned them about over and over. Borrowing heavy equipment for a cleanup without permission was no exception.

The crew chief jumped out of the helicopter and met them. He asked, "Did you ride out the storm here?"

"Yep! But it wasn't our choice. We were kind of stranded." Rock told him.

Then the crew chief told him, "I'll notify Galveston PD and have someone come and get you. I hope you know, they probably won't make it until tomorrow."

Rock spoke up loudly, "Wait minute! We fished six people out of the debris. All of them on the elderly side."

The crew chief was also a medic, and immediately walked over to the shack and checked on the seniors. He was impressed with how Rock and Runner had taken care of them, but stated that he couldn't take any of them with him in the helicopter. They were all safe and no one was majorly injured. Rescue would be the next day.

The Coast Guard notified the Galveston Police Department and then Officer Ray came by the house and gave Mama the good news. Rock and Runner were alive and well. Mama was relieved. That night she finally got some sleep.

Shortly after the Coast Guard helicopter left, the sun went down and it got dark fast. All the electricity to the islands were severed, so there wasn't a single street or house light to be seen anywhere. It was too dark to work anymore. Rock and Runner went back to the cabin and managed to scrounge enough to make a meal for everyone. When they finished, everyone fell asleep.

The next morning Rock and Runner were back on the dozer and backhoe, pushing the debris off the roads and piling it on the side.

Runner found a little white dog wandering about the debris. It was so tired, it let Runner pick him up without the slightest bark, just a whimper. That was another miracle.

The rescuing forced Rock and Runner to think about what else might be out there, more specifically, people that needed to be rescued.

After Runner walked up the stairs to the beach cabin, he handed the little dog to the seniors. That seemed to lift their spirits. It was obvious the old folks recognized the dog and the dog recognized them.

Runner stared at the old people as they petted the dog and rejoiced. I think both my brothers were a little mesmerized by the scene.

Runner turned to his brother, "Rock, maybe we better get on the backhoe, and make a quick trip around the city."

"See if anyone else survived?" Rock asked.

"Yeah. There's no one else to look, brother, just us."

Rock nodded his head, "I'm with you."

Rock and Runner took the backhoe around the outskirts of the town. It didn't take long. Crystal City was not that big.

Before they decided to head back to the helipad area, they came upon one unusual looking debris pile on the west side of the town. Curiosity made them get off the backhoe and look on the other side. When they did, they were shocked to see giant piles of dead cattle, washed up in long drifts and starting to bloat.

The surge from *Ike* had pushed inland and flooded all the pastures, bringing the water level halfway up to the cows' chests. The ones that didn't drown, drank the brackish water and quickly died. There were hundreds of cattle found floating in giant drifts along the fence corners and tree lines.

It was a terrible sight for my brothers to see. That cattle ranch was the only neighbor to the north that the city had.

Although my brothers weren't cowboys, they knew in an instant that this was a loss for everyone, especially that ranch. They also knew that the dead cow problem was too big for them to handle, so they headed back to the cabin.

The next day Rock and Runner got straight to work on their dozer and backhoe. They were within a hundred yards of each other, working in unison, pushing what looked like the remainder of the debris into neat piles and rows to be ready for pickup by FEMA contractors that they knew would be there later.

My brothers had considered this fun for the first hour after they got the machines running, but it had quickly turned into work. From the day before and until late that morning, they valiantly acknowledged it to be work, and what's more, they stayed with it blindly, not knowing where or when the end would be.

That morning their excursion came to a head. While Rock and Runner were pushing debris, they both looked up at about the same time and saw a group of men watching them. It was two deputy sheriffs, a few rescue workers, and probably the most shocking, the owner of the machines they were running. He was the same big white man they were watching at the construction site a few days before, and he didn't look happy. They finally learned who he was. His name was Buck Patterson.

There is no telling how long Mr. Patterson had been watching, but when Rock and Runner saw him, they pulled their machines out of the debris piles, lowered the blades to the ground and killed the engines. Then they got down and walked over to Mr. Patterson, both still wearing their plastic hardhats and safety vests.

Rock and Runner extended their hands and gave the keys to Mr. Patterson.

"Here's your keys," Rock said.

Then Runner added, "There's no water in the crank-cases and all the joints were kept greased."

All Buck Patterson could do was say, "Thanks, son."

Then one of the deputies said something that was more of a statement looking for verification than a question, "You know what kind of trouble you're in?"

Runner just glanced at the ground, "Yes, sir. I guess we do."

"I'm kind of looking forward to some jailhouse food... Let someone else do the cooking for a change," Rock told them. "I don't think we had enough to feed everybody one more time anyway."

The deputy asked, "What do you mean everybody?"

Rock pointed to the only structure left, the metal cabin on pipe stilts, "We found six survivors, old people in the debris after the storm, dressed their wounds, and then took them all up there."

It was impossible to know what Mr. Patterson and the deputies were thinking. Mr. Patterson later described it as, "A group of first responders, all with looks of disbelief on their faces." Disbelief that two young boys not yet out of high school, took charge of a bad situation and maintained it until rescuers got there.

Finally they broke their stupor and got to work. The rescue squad took care of the senior citizens. Buck Patterson disappeared, and the deputies took Rock and Runner to the sheriff's office. They were not handcuffed.

Rock and Runner made bail for everything they had done wrong. Not only did they miss the county bus, which was a violation of their probation, but now there was a new charge of unauthorized use of a motor vehicle, or in this case, a bulldozer and backhoe.

Then time passed. It was almost as if the courts forgot about everything, but it was not to be.

Three months later on the day of the trial, we all showed up to court not knowing what to expect. Mama was in her best dress and all her sons were smartly and properly attired.

Everyone agreed that considering all the facts, these were ridiculous charges at the very least, but the county prosecutor wouldn't have it. He wanted a conviction to hang his hat on for the taking of the dozer and backhoe.

Once the County Judge found out that Rock and Runner had helped rescue the heart attack victim and his son on the fishing boat, he declined it as a violation of probation. The fact that they had missed the bus was a frivolous detail compared to their good deed. The County Judge dismissed those charges.

But the unauthorized taking of the dozer and backhoe was a different story, and the county attorney was ordered to prosecute the case in district court as a felony. That meant Rock and Runner wouldn't be in front of the County Judge, they would be in front of a district judge, and that made all the difference in the world. It was the difference between a little jail time and county probation, and a prison sentence in Huntsville, Texas.

As we waited in the halls of the courthouse, we couldn't help but overhear a commotion behind the door of the jury room. It was a heated argument between two men. I leaned next to the door and got an earful.

The argument was between the County Attorney and Buck Patterson. Before I could get anything out of the conversation, the court was called into session. Everyone went inside and sat down. Rock and Runner sat down in the front with their public defender.

Immediately after the judge sat down, Buck Patterson spoke up loudly, "Your Honor, could I approach the bench?"

"And who are you?" the judge asked.

"My name is Buck Patterson. The owner of the equipment these boys are being prosecuted for," Patterson replied.

As Buck approached the bench, the prosecutor and defender followed him to the bench.

"Make this quick, Mr. Patterson, we're about to hold court," the judge said.

Then the Prosecutor spoke up, "Your Honor, Mr. Patterson wants to pull out of this case."

The judge asked Buck, "Is that true Mr. Patterson?"

"Yes sir, Judge. That's true," Buck replied.

"Mr. Patterson, the state has made the complaint against these men. All you're here for is to be a witness."

Then Buck Patterson laid everything on the line, "Yes sir. And when I take the stand I'm going to muddy up the case and deny everything. I won't cooperate."

The Judge pointed his finger at Buck and gave him a stern warning, "You do that and I'll find you in contempt... maybe have charges of perjury filed against you."

In defiance, Buck Patterson squinted his eyes, leaned in closer and stunned him with his answer, "A little time in jail wouldn't hurt me. I could use the vacation."

The defending attorney's jaw was on the floor, "You're crazy," he told Buck.

They all stared at each other for a moment. Then the judge asked the defense, "What do you think, counselor?"

"I'm all for it. Of course."

Buck explained in detail, "Look, Your Honor, those boys dug my equipment out of a debris pile. Then when no one asked them to, they went to work. They cleared over twenty miles of roads and the helipad at Crystal Beach for Christ sakes! Oh and let's not forget, they pulled six old people from the carnage over there and tended to their needs for a day and a half until they were all rescued. Does that sound like the criminal mind to you?"

Then the defense added, "Your Honor. Right before the hurricane hit, they helped pull a heart attack victim from the surf and put him in an ambulance. That's why they missed the county bus and were stuck on the other side... and they rescued a dog."

The judge looked at the prosecutor and asked, "A dog? Is this all true?"

The prosecutor nodded his head yes.

Buck took a second breath of air and started again, "I had a long time to think about this, Judge. And I knew I'd be walking a thin line if I decided to do this, but this ain't right. There's no justice if these boys get sent up to Huntsville. They'll lose faith in the system, and so would I."

"What do you say to that, Mr. Prosecutor?" the judge asked.

The prosecutor just rubbed his face and sighed. It was a great disappointment to him. "I guess so."

The judge lightly tapped his gavel on the bench, "So be it. In the interest of justice, this case is dismissed."

Rock and Runner were spared any possible sentence that day. Mama was spared a grieving breakdown and I was simply relieved. The boys were almost made heroes when it was over. Uncle Bud and Officer Ray made it point to shake their hands for doing the right thing under impossible circumstances. That was just the boost my brothers needed.

A year later, Rock and Runner graduated high school. Out of the blue, Buck Patterson called the house and offered them jobs. That's right. He gave them jobs operating his heavy equipment. Now they go to work every day and make money without taking shortcuts.

My brothers aren't here to wheel me around anymore. They started lives of their own. I consider it a small price to pay for their success. It was a good sacrifice and I've never been more proud of them.

When I graduate high school, I doubt that my path will be the same. Maybe I'll be a scientist, or a doctor. I know I can do it because I was always the smart one. And my brain is as big as a watermelon.

Texas Clam Bake

I HAD BEEN WORKING in Iraq for the last eight years. Not as a soldier, but as a construction worker for the Department of Defense. We rebuilt the country the best we could and as fast as we could, but when we got back to the States, they tore it all up again. Oh well, we did the best we could. War and internal strife—not only does it kill people but it tears things up faster than you can drive a nail.

Now it was time to work here at home, in Texas. My initial plan was to save enough money to start my own construction company when I got back. I did, but before I started my new construction company, I needed some rest and relaxation out at my old hangout, Patty's Bar and Grill.

Patty's was the place that the locals went to hang out. The only problem was that I had been gone so long, I wasn't sure if any of my friends would still be there, or even recognize me for that matter. All the same, I missed my friends, even the obnoxious ones.

Late one Saturday afternoon I decided to go to Patty's. Still daylight, I saw a few vehicles and about ten motorcycles in the gravel parking lot. Everything looked the same as I left it on the outside. The signs were still blinking and I could hear the music thumping inside.

Before I could get to the back door, a commotion caught my attention in the back of the parking lot. It was a fight. A fight between four "want to be badass" male bikers and four biker dykes—and the dykes were kicking their ass.

I don't know what started it, but the first man I saw was lying motionless on the ground. Of course he could have been sleeping, except for that raised knot on his forehead. One of those sweet little lesbians had whopped him good.

"Poor guy," I was thinking to myself, "he was sleeping through all the excitement." For that matter, I could see right away these boys were not very good at this fighting thing.

The biggest of the lesbians had a headlock on the second man. She was force-feeding him handfuls of dirt she scooped from the ground. During a lull in the force-feeding he tried to spit out the dirt, so she took her knuckles and gave him a long and continuous noogie until a patch of hair fell out of his head.

Lesbian number two had wrestled her victim to the ground and had him in some kind of mixed martial arts leg lock. Every time she torqued down on his leg, he would holler in pain.

Of course, the most gruesome of the fights was what the remaining two lesbian bikers were doing to the last of the proud men bikers. One of the girls had him in a choke hold while the fourth lesbian was yanking on his testicles. It looked like she was trying to start a lawn mower or something. It hurt me just to watch. I never knew that a man's testicles could stretch that far out without popping off the body.

That's when I noticed that the lesbian that was yanking on the crank was my old friend, Penny. Even though I had been gone for eight years, this was a surprise. I never knew she rode motorcycles, much less did I ever think she would become a gang leader of killer lesbians.

A part of me wanted to feel sorry for these old boys, but that inner voice told me that they probably deserved everything they were getting, so I decided not to get involved. With all the screams for mercy going on, this was definitely a setback for the machismo of men. This was one fight they were not going to brag about.

Oh well, I was sure that they could eventually sort it out, so I traded their entertainment for another and went inside.

There was a fair-sized crowd when I went through the doors, but I didn't recognize anyone except the bartender, Catarina. Cat, as her friends called her, was the bartender when I left. She still had that killer body that would make men buy beer and stare at her until they reached the land of stupid.

Cat filled me in on how the bar had changed since I was there. She said that most of the old crowd still came in, although most came in early because they all had jobs and were dodging DWIs. The major change was that the bar was now a biker hangout. That was obvious.

After a few minutes, Penny and her three companions came through the door, all sweaty and breathing heavy. They were still pumped up from winning that fight. Yes, they were an intimidating looking bunch.

Penny walked up to me and stuck out her hand, "Matt. How the hell are you?"

I got a hug out of her instead.

"I'm back in one piece, which is more than I can say for those guys outside," I told her.

Penny wasn't a natural hater of men when I left, but I feared that something had changed. Something told me that her and her gang had developed a taste for blood. Anything with a penis was probably a potential target. When I had left, Penny was what I called pretty. Now she looked like a Marine right out of boot camp.

She apologized immediately, "I'm sorry you had to see that, Matt. We had to take care of some business. Sit with us. Let's catch up."

I didn't mind sitting down with Penny so much, but those other three soldiers gave me concern. They spent the next minute congratulating each other on their win with high fives and short recreations of the fight. Then they sucked their first beers down like a bunch of sailors on liberty and took turns staring at me across the table. It was a look of pure disdain.

My mother referred to their kind as clam lickers. Of course in her day I seriously doubt she was referring to the militant types. Now I found myself in the situation where I was supposed to have a conversation with them? It was going to be like trying to pet three pit bulls that didn't know you. A man could lose a finger doing that. I had to watch what I said. After all, I liked my testicles right where they were, my hair on my head, and my leg functional.

Penny and I made small talk for a while. Then we suddenly realized we had all run out of beer. That's when Penny got up from the table and went to the bar to get more, leaving me with her three killer lesbians.

As soon as she walked away, the big one they called Bridgett, leaned in and looked at me and asked in a nasally voice, "What are you looking at? Ain't you never seen a lesbian before?"

I successfully fought back the urge to snicker at her voice. It was a good thing I did too. Whatever came out of my mouth next had to be done with tact and forethought. "Sure I have. Of course, they weren't ripping the gonads off of men at the time."

"They weren't gentlemen!" Linda shouted at me. "They didn't approve of the way we live. What's more, they thought we were helpless pushovers... called us names. Then they got rude."

Then Sue, third dyke leaned in, still pumped, "What about you? You got any beef about the way we are?"

I was fascinated with Sue. She had a mouse face, and could have been classified as cute in my book. "Calm down girls," I told them as I leaned away from them. "I'm here with you... on your side."

"That's good," Bridgett told me sternly. "Let's keep it that way... and don't be making goo-goo eyes at Penny. She's my woman."

"Things have changed a little since I've been away, but when I left, Penny and I were friends. Nothing more."

"Where you been?" Sue asked.

"Iraq."

"They have any lesbians in Iraq?" She continued.

"None that I ran in to. Of course all the women were covered in bed sheets, from head to toe."

When Penny came back to the table I breathed a sigh of relief. I hoped that we could now segue into more civilized conversation. And we did; for the next hour we talked, drank beer, and had a good time. But have no illusions about the setting. I wasn't one of them, as I found out with that occasional "go-to-hell" look I got from each one of them.

At one point, Penny was telling a story about the old days, how we would drink all day around a campfire and then go skinny-dipping in the river.

"You got naked and went swimming with boys?" Linda asked Penny.

Penny was smiling, "Yep. The first time I took my clothes off and jumped in the river, I think Matt freaked."

Bridgett asked me, "You saw Penny naked?"

"Of course," I cautiously told her. "We were skinny dipping."

As the conversation continued, Bridgett got my attention and pulled me to the side. Her voice changed to a meeker tone, "Okay. Then maybe you could help me with a problem I'm having."

Bridgett was asking a friendly question. Something only friends did. Despite me wanting to laugh every time she spoke in that nasally voice, I had to take advantage of this bonding opportunity. "If I can, sure," I politely accommodated her.

Then Bridgett let me have it, "I've been trying to convince Penny to trim that tarantula of hers. It's so hairy, I could weave a rope."

My body wrenched, "Oh, my god! Don't tell me that!" It was like she was talking about my sister.

"I'm serious," Bridgette continued. "The other day I coughed up a hairball—one of those hairs was long enough to floss my teeth."

"Stop!" I begged her. "You're going to give me nightmares! No more."

"Bridgett!" Penny yelled. "What the hell are you telling him? You bitch! Where's your manners?"

While the two of them went straight into a minor lover's quarrel, I noticed a single woman come through the door out of the corner of my eye. It wasn't anyone I knew, so I dismissed the entry and continued to drink.

However, Sue recognized her and went into alarm mode. She got every one's attention and shouted a whisper, "Don't look now, but we got trouble! Brenda just walked through the door."

In unison, all four repositioned their chairs at the table, lowered their heads, and huddled in close. I was right in the middle of their huddle and it was obvious they wanted to be inconspicuous. None of them would look up, much less look towards the woman at the door. The atmosphere had changed quickly.

At that instant, I glanced at the one woman that had walked in, and then looked back at my new lesbian drinking buddies, cowering in their own self-made circle of fear.

"What in the holy hell is going on?" I asked. "It's only one girl... and she's rather beautiful."

"She's not what she appears to be," Sue told me in a concealed tone.

"She looks pretty normal to me," I told them.

"Sue's right. She's a hazard to everyone in this bar, especially us," Linda added. "Penny, what are we going to do?"

"Everybody keep your head down. Maybe she won't notice us and leave," Penny ordered.

I had to ask in a whisper, "I just watched you clean the clock on four men and none of you got a scratch. How is this so different? Why are we whispering?"

Penny leaned in and told me the story. "A couple of weeks ago we invited her to my house for a party. It had been raining all day and continued through the night. We were drinking and dancing and having fun, then suddenly she flipped out."

"Flipped out?" I asked.

"Yes. Flipped out. I don't know if it was the alcohol or she was on drugs or what, but she snapped and went crazy. She started tearing shit up for no reason. We tried to restrain her, but we couldn't hold her down. She caused eight hundred dollars in furniture damage alone. Not to mention what she did to us."

Then Bridgett sarcastically told her version, "Brenda, as lovely as she seems, picked me up above her head like she was one of those wrestlers on TV and lifted me into the ceiling fan... blades and glass went flying everywhere."

Sue continued, "Me and Linda tried to stop her, but she hurled me into a wall so hard I got stuck in the sheetrock and couldn't move."

"Oh come on! One woman against four?" I asked them in disbelief.

"I hit her in the head as hard as I could, but all it did was roll her eyes. The woman felt no pain," Linda said.

I turned to Penny, "Is that true?"

"Yeah, and that's only half the fight. She put me and Linda in head-locks and banged our heads together until I thought our eye balls were going to pop out of their sockets. She slung Linda across the room and took out the kitchen table and two chairs. Then she slapped me across the head so hard that everything went black. When I came to, I was outside in the rain being dragged through the mud by one leg like a wounded deer. Brenda had lost it. She was crying and screaming like a crazy person."

"What was she crying... or saying?"

Linda answered, "Nobody knows. Best we could figure, it was some kind of Slavic babble."

"Yeah, something that only demons can understand. The only thing that stopped her was a lightning strike on a nearby tree. When it happened, she dropped my leg and then walked off into the darkness, screaming and crying. That's the last time we saw her."

I watched as Brenda spotted the group of girls. She paused a moment, smiled, and slowly sashayed in our direction. The lesbian warriors were now as nervous as cats in a dog pound.

How should I describe Brenda? She certainly deserves one, so I'll try.

She was what I called voluptuous on a grand scale, standing about six feet tall, weighing about 175, and wearing a body-hugging dress that came half-way down her thighs. She wore high heels that made her a little taller than six foot, but nothing ridiculous. Her womanly build was a masterpiece of beauty, and yet her size was what I called big-boned. An Olympian type of figure that would make any man's head turn to look at those curves, and yet so often pass her by because of size intimidation.

I later found out she was actually from Poland. This girl had to be the descendant of Viking marauders back in some Nordic country. She immigrated to the States, decided to stay, and then evidently became a bisexual predator. No wonder my lesbian buddies were scared of her. She was twice as big as any one of them.

When Brenda reached our table, she was carrying a mixed drink with a tiny umbrella from the bar. "Hello, girls," she said with a slight accent.

It was only then that their heads looked up, submissively.

"Hi, Brenda." Penny answered.

"Can I sit here?" Brenda asked in a feminine tone.

Penny answered like she didn't have any choice. "Yes, ma'am," she said.

Brenda sat down on the other side of the table from me and I was suddenly overcome with more visual stimulation than I could handle. Her breasts were works of art, bulging out of the top of her dress like white freckled melons, slightly bouncing at will, causing a display of seismic ripples for everyone to see. You couldn't ignore them, no matter what species you were.

And that's not all. Her lips were enticingly full and plump. They were painted a glossy red and beckoned to be framed over some sex addict's fireplace. I tried not to show it, but I continued to stare. I had been in Iraq way too long.

Brenda tried to make small talk, but smooth conversation was not taking root. The other girls were scared and it was obvious. Then she got right to the business that was evidently bothering her from that infamous night.

"I want to apologize for my behavior the other night. I had a bad day... or night... or something. I really don't remember very much. Something set me off and I got a little angry."

"A little angry?" Bridgette blurted.

Penny grabbed Bridgette by the forearm to stop her from talking anymore. "That's all right, Brenda. We've all had bad days. That's the way things go sometimes."

I didn't hear much of the conversation. My concentration was diverted, as I was trying not to stare and make a spectacle of myself.

Brenda took a sip of her drink, looked at me and then asked, "Who's your friend, Penny?"

"This is my good friend, Matt. Matt, meet Brenda."

"Nice to meet you, Brenda. Heard a lot about you already..." All the gang gave me the you're-talking-too-much glance, "of course, it was all good."

Brenda replied with the sweetest and most feminine voice at the table, "Thank you, Matt. You must be one of those southern gentleman types. One does not encounter many gentlemen around here. It's a rare trait..." Then we watched her mind wander into a dark place, "sometimes churned up in a wake of chaos and floating in a sea of deceit and deception. I don't prescribe to those things of course. Transgressions give me jolts of livid upsurges."

Sue looked at Linda, "What the hell is she saying?"

"I have no idea," Linda replied.

Brenda was clearly talking above my lesbian buddies' heads. "Relax, girls. This is a process of reconciliation, if you will bear with me. I find it much more appealing than double vision or the sound of a cracking ulna."

All the lesbian dykes said, "Me too."

"It's just that nothings is falling into place lately. Everything I do seems to be wrong. I don't feel good. This morning I looked in the mirror and I couldn't stand the image I was looking at. I looked ugly. I felt ugly. I'm just an ugly person."

Without thinking, I jumped right in the middle of that firecracker stand with a lit cigarette, "You're not ugly. In fact, you're pretty."

That was the first time Brenda had smiled at the table. She glanced at me coyly, looked down at the table for a second, and slightly fluffed her hair. "Thank you, Matt. I have a feeling you truly are a nice man."

Time froze at that moment. While Brenda was bathing in the admiration I had given her, the lesbians were trying to stop my heart with their Vulcan mind stares. I knew they probably would've preferred me to keep quiet, but it was too late. All this time they were trying to uninvite Brenda to their table, and here I was doing exactly the opposite.

"Well, it's time for me to go, girls, while I feel good about myself." Brenda said and then downed the last of her drink.

A feeling of nervousness came upon the group as Brenda stood up and began to slowly walk around the table. All the lesbians placed their hands flat on the top of the table and never turned their heads. They were ready for the unexpected and I was with them.

"I'm going to go home and take a long hot bath," as she slowly walked around everyone and gently touched each one on the shoulder as she passed. "This has been a memorable night for me. While I like the theory of reconciliation and the execution of reprieves, nothing can pull a person out of a mental abyss... well you know... like flattery. Of course, it would also help if I didn't mix prescription medications with American whiskey."

At the end of that little speech, she was directly behind me. Without warning she bent my head over backwards and here came those fat ruby red lips. She planted a slurpy kiss dead center on my lips and gave me some unannounced tongue. While I was quickly running out of air, I couldn't help but notice she tasted like a combination of tequila and red hot candy. Saliva juices were starting to run down my jawline when she finally pulled off. I never resisted. The way I saw it, to try and stop a Viking when they're in the middle of passionate act could be a dangerous thing.

As soon as she stood back up she said, "Bye girls," and then walked out the door.

I grabbed a napkin and tried to clean myself up. I had red lipstick all over my mouth. To tell you the truth, I didn't know whether to be embarrassed or turned on about the incident. However, my lesbian biker friends did have an opinion.

All the girls leaned in very close and stared at me. No one would say a word. They just stared at me in what I guessed was amazement.

Finally, I as asked them, "Something the matter?"

"How was it?" asked Bridgette.

"Kind of wet... and slimy," I told her.

"You're probably a quart low on blood but don't know it yet." Sue said.

"I feel kind of dizzy to tell you the truth... and thirsty," I told them.

Then Penny looked me straight in the eyes and said, "I've never seen anything like it. That was absolutely the bravest thing."

"No shit, Matt." Bridgette said with a smile, "You just French-kissed a rattlesnake and lived to tell about it."

Linda patted me on the shoulder, "You didn't even get bit. You're my new hero."

For the rest of the night these lesbian bikers venerated me to hero status. It was quite the treatment and a boost to my ego. I gained three friends and a disturbed stalker out of the whole deal. That was an accomplishment.

As time went by, I became good friends with all of the girls. They are my lesbian support team. Now, when we get together I call our parties a Texas Clam Bake, to give credit to my late mother, of course.

As for Brenda "The Terrible," we all see her from time to time, and, as all of us do, we are inevitably on the way to somewhere else when it happens. When Penny and her gang are invited to Brenda's house for drinks, they always seem to be leaving on a long biker's road trip—of course.

I run interference for them when I can, but I've got my own problems with her. Eventually Brenda's going to figure out that I never left the States for a second trip to Iraq. That taste of tequila and red hot candy is not something that goes away easily.

Recently, I read a San Antonio news article about a man that jumped off a bridge into the cold waters of the San Antonio River in the middle of winter. He didn't get hurt from the fall, but suffered hyperthermia from floating down the river about a quarter mile before he decided to get out. Eventually he crawled out through the mud and the brush to the only house he could find that had a light on to seek help.

The man told police that after he met this rather beautiful and large blonde girl in a bar, they decided to take it to a motel. Somewhere in the midst of their short relationship things went very wrong.

Out of his head from the loss of body heat and being totally spent from crawling through the brush, he gave an interesting final quote to the San Antonio Express newspaper:

> *...then she put on a helmet with horns and went crazy.*
> *She chased me down a dark street while trying to hit me with a*
> *nine iron. I had to jump in the river to save my life...*

Hmmm... I wonder who that could have been?

73

She's No Barbie

I FOUND MYSELF sitting at the kitchen table and staring at the wall, stewing in my own little corner of darkness and wondering how far I would sink. It was one of the lowest times in my life.

My wife had picked up and left while I was at work and it broke my heart. Knowing that I wasn't the only man that this had ever happened to was no comfort either. She didn't leave as a result of infidelity or anger between us. Her reason was rather unique.

She had been gone for only one day, but I missed my wife terribly. That is, if she was still my wife. For all I knew, she was going to file for an annulment or something. It would have helped if she had told me something before she left.

There was a small part inside me that didn't blame her for leaving. At least that's what I told people when they asked. I suppose her first reason for disliking our lifestyle started with our first house, a dumpy looking, single-wide trailer in the middle of the South Texas desert.

We lived less than fifty miles from the Mexican border and had no close neighbors. Every day the temperature would hit one hundred degrees and our house was surrounded by a wilderness of dangerous obstacles. There were a variety of plants and animals that had the capabilities to bite, sting, poison, cling to, and suck the life out of the average city person in moments. That included rattlesnakes, coyotes, mountain lions, wild hogs, vinegaroons, all kinds of cacti, and those ever-present grass burrs.

Nothing bothered me of course. I was having fun playing *Walker, Texas Ranger*. What could possibly go wrong?

When I dragged my Barbie-type away from her metro world and across our tarantula-infested yard, I watched the look in her eyes, and it wasn't good.

One morning Paige yelled her thoughts on the matter, "This country is uninhabitable for decent human beings, Henry! There's dust everywhere and this morning I found grass burrs in my best pair of panties."

"You found a what?" acting like I didn't understand.

She sat down on the arm of the couch. "You heard me... grass burrs. Doesn't do any good to throw them out the door. They just grow a new plant wherever they land. I think they're growing in the carpet."

"You want me to pick up some grass burr killer?" I asked.

She continued her indignant complaints. "No. You know I can't even go outside without fear of having a heat stroke or getting the eye from those damn lizards."

That caught my attention. "What the hell? You got a complaint about the lizards?"

The look on her face showed me she was serious. "Oh yeah! When I walk out the door they run up to me, cock their little heads, and look at me with their beady little eyes. I don't know what they're thinking."

"They're reptiles, Paige. Quit trying to read their minds."

Then she plopped down on the couch and told me the real problem. "I have no friends and this place is torture, Henry. All day long I sit here and do nothing."

I didn't know what to say. Not really. "Give it some time, Sweetheart. Think of yourself as a pioneer woman, blazing a trail through unexplored territory."

That little speech didn't go over too well.

I took my first job out of the academy as a deputy sheriff in an isolated town called Dry Wells. The county provided our house for free, but it was four bump gates and eleven miles from the nearest town, so the situation left little chance for Paige to socialize with anyone. That made her that much more lonesome.

Before long, Ginger, the little dog that Paige grew up with disappeared; it was never to be seen again. We both finally concluded that a rattlesnake killed it out in the brush somewhere. Rattlesnakes were everywhere.

Then she got a second little dog, and named it Selina. It disappeared like the first, leaving no clue as to what had happened.

On her third dog, named Cookie, while keeping a close watch through the window while it peed in the yard, Paige watched as a coyote ran out of the brush, grabbed the little dog around the midsection, and shook it like a rat. Without putting on her shoes, Paige charged out the door carrying her mop, but it was too late. Cookie was taken away as a coyote dinner.

Owning a small dog in a country thick with coyotes is like throwing a grasshopper in a pond full of hungry fish. Once the grasshopper hits the surface of the water, there's a slim chance of it making it back to the bank.

Paige was on the living room floor when I returned home. She was picking the grass burrs off every part of her body. Little mud streaks had formed down her cheeks where her tears had drooled and dried. My first inclination was to laugh, but better judgment took hold of me. She was an emotional mess. I tried to console her, giving her what I thought was the most obvious explanation to the problem.

"Honey! Let's face it, all the dogs had wimpy names. We'll get a fourth dog and give it a macho name. That should do the trick."

"I don't want another dog, Henry," as she scolded me through her muddy teeth. "I hate this place." She started to cry, "I don't think I can take it anymore."

That last part put the shivers down my spine. Here we were barely six months married, and she was already talking about quitting.

I took off my gun belt, laid it on the couch, and gently sat on the floor next to her. The rest of the day and most of that night, I did my best to convince her that things weren't that bad. It wasn't easy, but after some time she decided she would give it one more shot.

That night, when things had settled down, a frightening reality sat in. She might leave me anyway, no matter what I said or did. Paige was a city girl from the Dallas/Fort Worth area, so she never grew up having, let's say, challenging days. She was beautiful and perfect. She could have been a magazine model that chased the glittering lights, but yet chose to marry me.

In Dry Wells, she discovered her only purpose now was that of the good wife who stayed at home. I never intended it to be that way. Pretty boring I must admit. So, I made some concessions.

I taught Paige how to shoot a pistol and then a shotgun. That had to be the first order of business, even though her first shot put a hole in the bed of my truck. This was the first time in her life that learning how to handle a gun was going to keep the wolves off the porch.

I bought her another dog too. It was a full-grown blue heeler, complete with a bad attitude. I specifically picked the dog because I figured it had a slight mental illness. It was friendly towards people, but if you petted him too long, it would eventually start growling and looking for something to bite. I named him Nail.

Nail bonded with Paige because she insisted on him being the alpha of the group. Oddly enough, he also bonded with our cat, Flat Washer. Every time I came home, Nail would be raising holy hell at the door. He wanted to make sure that I knew he was on duty, and that was just the way I liked it.

As the days went by, we noticed that it had been five days since anyone had seen Flat Washer. While it's not uncommon for cats to wander for days from their homes seeking other cats, making small kills, and generally exploring the area they live, Flat Washer was overdue for a visit to the house.

One morning, after I had left for the office, Paige watched Nail freeze in place, his ears go straight up, and stare at the front door. Nail was listening to a pack of fighting coyotes not more than a hundred yards outside the house. They could both tell that the coyotes had cornered something in the brush.

Normally I would give Paige a low rating in the bravery department, but give her a dog like Nail and a loaded shotgun, and her ratings go up dramatically.

Paige did her best to ensure Nail kept close to her side, but when both of them rounded the last clump of brush, Nail couldn't stand it anymore and bolted away from her.

Paige was faced with five coyotes that had circled around a small ten-foot mesquite tree where Flat Washer was hanging on for his life. Fur was everywhere, and all of it belonged to Flat Washer. All of the hair, along with the skin on the cat's tail, was gone. The coyotes had evidently ripped it off, leaving about ten inches of tail bones sticking straight up into the air.

Nail attacked the coyotes, trying to protect Flat Washer or maybe Paige. We'll never really know. What we did know was that Nail latched onto one with his teeth and tore into his ass. That caused two more coyotes to jump in the fight against Nail. It was a situation of hair, blood, hide, screaming, and general chaos all at the same time.

Without giving much thought of aiming, Paige raised her shotgun and pulled the trigger in a panic, blowing off the main branch Flat Washer was clinging to. The cat fell straight down into the midst of the coyotes. The blast caused Nail to drop the one coyote, who proceeded to hightail it for the brush with the rest of his friends. About the same time, Flat Washer sprinted past Paige all the way back to the house.

Before the coyotes were out of sight, Paige managed to chamber another round and shoot into the brush. This time the recoil busted her lip from holding the gun too close to her face.

Paige managed to grab Nail by the collar and get back to the house. The episode was considered a win in my book, but the toll had frazzled her nerves.

When she returned home, her lip was bleeding and Flat Washer was screaming in pain from underneath her car. To make matters worse, there was a big thunderstorm about to hit the area. It was about to get hot and humid, making it extra miserable.

It was the threat of the storm and the first drops of rain that made Paige get down on her belly and crawl under the car to retrieve Flat Washer.

When she came out, she was filthy from head to toe with sweat, rain, and dirt stuck to every part of her body. Another pair of those rubber flip-flops were totally ruined, completely consumed by the grass burrs.

Paige tried to render first aid to Flat Washer's tail, but there was no way to bandage ten-inches of exposed bone. Then she tried to place an empty paper towel tube over the cat's tail, but Flat Washer would have none of it. It was too tender to touch. So she spent the next thirty minutes or so trying to get the kinks out of the cat's hair.

If that had been the end of the bad luck, then she might have been able to survive the day, but the thunderstorm knocked out the electricity, causing the trailer to heat up. Within the next hour the trailer was like an oven and the nearest shade was at least a mile away.

Since we were on a single well system, our leaky toilet quickly drained what water pressure we had and there was no way for her to clean up. That's when she said to herself, "Enough is enough." Then she packed up her things, Nail, and Flat Washer and left Dry Wells.

I found her flip-flops in the driveway. I found cat hair in various places. I also found the shotgun lying in the sand with the breach open and full of dirt. Then I found the note she left.

It was difficult to say what was in the letter since the paper was smeared with tears and mud. However, I could make out enough that my heart broke halfway through as I read on.

I was suddenly lost in my own house. That's where you found me at the beginning of this story.

Paige never said she was going to file for divorce, I just assumed it. So I tried to get mentally prepared. She wrote that she needed time to think. I didn't take that as encouraging news.

I woke up at about two in the morning, sitting at the kitchen chair, still dressed and in my gear. By the looks of things around me, I had been crying in my sleep. With all my strength, I forced myself to stand from the table and get cleaned up. Work at six o'clock was right around the corner.

I knew where she had gone, back to Dallas. I knew deep down that there was no use in calling her like the desperate heartbroken husband I really was.

The next afternoon when I walked in the door, the phone was ringing. It was Paige.

"Henry?" I heard her voice say.

My voice was shaking, but I had to ask, "Paige? Are you okay? Are you coming back home?"

"Yes, Henry, home," She told me, then paused long enough for me to start holding my breath. "The day I left... it was a bad day. I'll tell you all about it later."

"Good. You have no idea how worried I've been."

"Yeah. I knew you would be," trying to make me feel better. "But you know, Henry, I had to regroup. I'm bringing home some new gear and things."

"New gear?" I asked.

"You'll see... and by the way, you'll have to say goodbye to your ole 'Barbie' and hello to the new me."

I didn't know what the "new gear" thing meant. I was just glad she was coming back home.

No matter how hard I've tried to be a macho man in life, unfeeling or unconcerned with the intricacies of a relationship, I have never been any good at it. I love my wife deeply. To this very day, I don't know whether it is a good thing or bad. All I know is that my heart breaks at the drop of a hat.

★

The following Sunday afternoon, I could hear a vehicle coming down the gravel road, so I went out the front door.

Paige drove up in a Ford 250 four-wheel drive pickup that her father had helped her trade for her four-door Buick. It had a grill guard from hell on the front, big knobby tires, and a macho-looking four-wheeler in the back of the bed, complete with gun racks.

When she stepped out of the truck she was wearing high-top rattle-snake boots, a pair of sunglasses, and camo clothes to match. Paige looked like something right out of a modern hunting magazine.

To say the least, I smothered her with kisses and she returned the favor.

With more help from her father, she bought a new pistol that best suited the size of her hands. It was a semiautomatic .22 caliber and was pink in color. Then she pulled out a pink 20-gauge shotgun, also a better caliber for her frame. There was plenty of ammo too.

My wife had devised a plan. She was going to practice every day until the handling of the guns became second nature and she could hit anything she was aiming at.

Nail and Flat Washer were also back, although the vet had amputated the boney tail. Paige took that boney tail and kept it as a reminder of that day, of her pain and misery.

Her attitude had dramatically changed. Instead of continuing to fluff herself in the habits of a Barbie, she decided to adopt the camo world of the wild west. Her entire transformation was the result of a talk she had had with her grandmother, who luckily for me was still around.

Not only did Grandmother remind her of the duties and convictions of being a wife and taking the oath at the altar, but she told her of her own perils of being married long ago. Grandmother married the only man in Johnson County that didn't have running water. In those days, they only made it to town about one to two times a week, and hardship was an everyday affair.

The whole time Paige was gone, her anger grew at the thought of the situation that manipulated her into misery. She had come back home for a counterattack.

Every single day she practiced, whether I was home or not. She became a good shot. A very good shot. During the day her pink pistol and belt hung on the wall with loaded magazines and her pink shotgun lay by the door ready for action.

Every day when I went to work, she would load up her guns, get on her four-wheeler, put Nail on the back seat, and patrol the fifteen-hundred acres we lived on from one windmill to another for coyotes and other critters.

During the next two months, she managed to kill one coyote while it was on the run with her .22 pistol. Normally this gun would not do the job except at close range, but she hit it in the head, so I praised her for it.

When she brought the coyote back to the house, she was so proud and excited I thought she was going to make me cook it on the grill to consummate the kill. We might have had to, except the coyote was infested with a bad case of fleas. Everyone got infested—me, Paige, Nail, and Flat Washer.

Winter in that part of South Texas is not like other parts of the state. When it is a generally uncomfortable forty degrees here, other northern parts of the state can be well into the freezing marks with snow and ice.

We had plenty of deer to pick for fresh meat, as well as wild hogs, quail, and white-winged dove to harvest. I seldom hunted anymore unless it was something big like a deer. Especially since Paige was so adamant about killing some kind of varmint every day. She always had something to eat when I came home. This was all of her own choice as it became her sport and I was always proud of her. Life was good.

Paige had found herself, but the incident put the scare in me. I would occasionally ask myself, "Could I give her everything she wanted?" After all, there was one more thing that was bound to come up—she had no social life.

Early spring always brought out a sudden influx of illegal aliens from Mexico. Most of them wanted jobs. They wanted to escape the drug cartels. They wanted hospitals to treat their children so they didn't die from things like tuberculosis or simple infections. You couldn't blame them. The problem was ever-present and undeniable.

However, the biggest threats were the illegal aliens coming over the border as mules, packing drugs across the river. No secondary crime was off-limits in order to make their deliveries, and this always gave me a worry. The Border Patrol did their best, but they never caught them all.

During mid-February the sheriff sent me to Del Rio to deliver a prisoner to the Val Verde County Jail. I wasn't due back home until later that night. So before I left, I gazed at my wife one last time as she lay there in bed, ever so motionless and beautiful.

An hour later, Paige hit the floor running. After fixing a quick breakfast for herself and Nail, she put on her high-top boots and pistol and left the house fully loaded. This was a routine that Nail knew well and looked forward to every morning. Nail got to ride on the back of Paige's four-wheeler while she zipped up and down the trails.

This morning's weather was to be typical for the time of year. It started out cold in the morning, but was warming up fast. These were also ideal conditions for immigrants to cross the border.

Her first stop was at the southern water trough where she got off the four-wheeler to look for signs. Paige had gained enough experience to know that something was different that morning, and she was right. There were human footprints in the mud all around the first water trough.

Paige's concern at that point was exactly what I had told her, make sure none of them were in physical trouble and that they veered away from the house, not towards it. The Border Patrol could handle the rest.

She drove to the next water trough, stopped a hundred yards short, parked the four-wheeler, and decided to walk forward very quietly. As she approached it, she watched Nail trot up to a bundle of rags that was lying in the grass and start licking it. When Paige rolled the bundle over, she was shocked at what she saw. It was a baby boy, not more than six months old.

"Oh, my God!" she said to herself.

It didn't take a doctor to see that the baby was dehydrated and on the edge of death. The baby's little eyes were open and glazed over, it's mouth open and gasping for air.

She picked it up and walked over to the water trough, where the freshest water was coming out of the float. With her fingers cupped just right, Paige managed to get some water into the baby's mouth, a trickle at a time. That did the trick. The baby started to respond and shortly began to look more alive.

Seeing life come back into the baby eased Paige's urgency, but not her curiosity. "What in the world is a little Mexican baby doing... left in the grass?" She asked Nail, as he stared at her and the baby.

Within seconds, faint cries came out of the brush. It was a woman's voice. It was the cries of distress. It was the kind of noises that came from a fight.

As quickly as she could, she placed the baby strategically in the shade next to the water trough and drew her pistol. Before she left she sternly looked at Nail, "Stay, Nail. Watch the baby." Nail stayed.

Paige sneaked through the brush until she found where all the noise was coming from. It was five illegals, two men and three women.

Paige learned later that all of the women, Silvia, Maria, and Juanita all knew each other. The girls had decided to cross the Rio Grande together with these men, as they thought there would be safety in numbers. But they had picked the wrong hombres. The men were known as "The Brothers" and they were bad to the bone.

When the group had reached the second water trough, the brothers decided they were refreshed enough to take liberties with at least two of the girls.

The women had fought them off the best they could and then finally ran in all directions to get away. Somewhere in the process, one of the men had taken the baby Juanita was carrying and slung it to the ground to be left in the sun. This was the baby that Paige found laying in the brush.

By the time Paige walked up on the situation, the two Brothers had beaten all three girls to a pulp and Brother number one was about to have his way with Maria.

When Paige saw what was happening, she walked boldly into the scene with her pistol pointed at the man. She knew exactly what was going on, and the fact that a rape was about to happen in front of her caused Paige to become enraged.

"Get off of her, you son-of-a-bitch!" Paige demanded. "So help me... I'll blow your head clean off if you don't get off."

The Brothers were completely caught off guard. They slowly stood up with their mouths gaping. Brother number one slowly pulled up his pants and looked at Paige.

"Look. It's a crazy gringa with a little gun," he said.

Then the second Brother took a step towards her, trying to hide a stick behind his leg, "A little... pink gun."

As the second Brother drew back his stick, Paige promptly put a bullet in his thigh. No hesitation. The hollow point left a nice bloody hole for him to tend to.

When the first Brother saw this, he quickly pulled a knife from his belt and stabbed Paige in the shoulder. But before he could pull the knife out, she drilled three quick rounds into the middle of his chest. Still able to stand, he staggered backwards leaving the knife in her shoulder, looked at her, and tried to laugh.

Paige could see right away, that those three shots to the chest didn't do the job. So she aimed the pistol straight at his head.

"Paco will see you in hell!" Brother number one growled in defiance, then collapsed to the ground.

All three of the Mexican girls immediately scrambled to their feet to help Paige. They didn't know who she was, but their instincts told them it didn't matter. All they knew was that Paige helped them out of a terrible situation.

Within seconds, the girls pulled the knife from Paige's shoulder and started jabbering in Spanish. Paige understood little, but did understand *bambino*, which meant baby.

"*Yo tango bambino.*" Paige told the one girl. "Follow me."

Before they left the area, wounded Brother number two started to scream obscenities in Spanish towards the girls. He kept screaming until they were out of range.

Nail had done his job and the baby was still safe. When the girls arrived, Nail was surrounded by six cows that were trying to get a drink from the water trough. He kept them at bay all that time.

The baby belonged to Juanita and she was very happy to see her child again. Juanita smothered Paige with praises, but her thank-yous were quickly overshadowed by the alarming tone Silvia and Maria had as they kept trying to tell Paige something she couldn't understand. It was something important and urgent. That much was for certain, but it was Spanish at ninety-miles per hour.

Then Silvia remembered some English. "Many brothers, very bad," she said as she pointed to the brush.

It became obvious to Paige in an instant. There were more Brothers of the ones she shot somewhere in the brush, and they evidently weren't good-natured. Brother number two, with the bullet in his leg, had tried to tell them that during their exit from the crime scene.

As soon as they reached the four-wheeler, Paige had to decide who to quickly take to the house and who to leave behind. So losing blood and slowly losing her strength, Paige motioned for Juanita and the baby to get on the four-wheeler.

Then she turned to Maria and Silvia and pointed down to the four-wheeler tracks, "Follow the road."

Silvia looked at her intensely trying to understand, "*Como?*"

Paige pointed towards the house again, "Follow the road! Find the house! *Mira la casa! Me casa!*"

Silvia's face showed she understood, then spoke up, "Oh, yes. *Su casa.* I understand."

Then Paige looked at Nail and pointed at him, "Stay Nail. Stay with the girls."

The plan was to race back to the house, and come back with the pickup to get Silvia and Maria.

After Paige hit the gas and was driving down the trail, she started to get dizzy from all the blood loss. About a mile down the trail, she slowed down considerably. Juanita took notice and caught her before she completely passed out and fell off the four-wheeler. After the four-wheeler came to a stop and died, Juanita took a closer look. Paige had lost too much blood and was unconscious.

Juanita didn't know how to drive a four-wheeler. All she had ever done was watch people drive them, that's all. But as luck would have it, they were close enough that she could see the top of a house through the mesquite about a half a mile away. Juanita knew that roof had to be the house Paige told them about. Juanita also knew that she couldn't carry both Paige and her baby back to the house at the same time. Leaving either one alone in the heat would invite certain death. She wasn't going to risk either one of them.

Juanita bravely jumped into the driver's seat and piddled and farted around with the controls until she accidentally hit the starter and the machine jumped. A few more tries and she got it going. She drove the whole way to the house in first gear, but she did it.

In a frantic mess, Juanita carried Paige inside the house where it was cool from the air conditioning. Then she ran out to the four-wheeler again and grabbed her baby and laid it on the couch next to Paige.

Paige started to regain consciousness about that time, but was still very woozy. She looked at Juanita. "The keys to my truck," pointing to the wall next to the door. Then she passed out again.

Juanita knew how to drive a truck. She jumped in Paige's truck and drove as fast as she could through the desert, trying frantically to get to Silvia and Maria before the Brothers did.

A matter of time was lost for Paige. When she finally came to, the sun was going down on the horizon. The girls had cleaned and bandaged her shoulder very nicely. What had awakened her from her unconsciousness was the yelling commotion at the front door.

Juanita was giving someone a good cussing in Spanish while holding Paige's shotgun on one of the Brothers.

Paige managed to get up and look out the window. There were six men there, all the infamous Brothers, with nothing more than clubs and knives as weapons, and they wanted Paige for revenge.

"The Brothers?" she asked Silvia.

"Two are Brothers, four are *cabróns,*" Silvia said with a stiff upper lip.

"Criminals," Maria added.

The head Brother told Juanita, in Spanish, that they only wanted the white girl, nothing more, and if they gave her up the rest could go unharmed.

After the ordeal Juanita, Silvia, and Maria had been through, they unanimously decided they were going to make a stand. Instead of surrendering Paige, they hurled more insults at the Brothers and wouldn't let any of them near the door.

Somewhere during the verbal exchange, Nail managed to get out the door. Although Paige yelled for Nail to stop, he ran down the steps of the porch and latched onto one of the Brother's legs. Immediately two more Brothers beat Nail with their clubs until he took a head shot and Nail went limp.

All three of the girls immediately came out of the house, armed and dangerous. Juanita and Silvia had Paige's pink guns and Maria had the handle of a mop. The Brothers could immediately sense the determination these girls suddenly had. When one of the Brothers lifted his club for a final swing on Nail, Juanita fired a shotgun round at his feet so he could feel the dust splatter his pants.

They walked down the porch steps, all gleaming with what horse traders refer to as the "crazy eye." When a horse is so dangerous and unpredictable that you can't saddle or ride him. That made the Brothers walk backwards as the girls came down to Nail. Juanita and Silvia put the barrels of their guns right in the Brothers' faces and dared them to do something stupid.

The Brothers knew the "crazy eye." It forced them to suddenly contemplate their own life expectancy. It occurred to them that they could be killed at any second by these crazy Mexican women with guns. These women were *loco*.

While the Brothers were contemplating being shot, Maria gently picked Nail up and brought him into the house.

Paige described the girls as transforming into militant killers from the age of Pancho Villa, like eighteenth-century Mexican revolutionaries. The only thing missing was sombreros and loaded bandoliers. They had pulled together and become a force to be reckoned with, all fear of the Brothers now a fleeting afterthought. They weren't about to give up or give in. Their objective had, without a second thought, changed from getting across the border to protecting Paige.

They had put everything on the line and sacrificed their futures for the young white girl that had saved them. For they knew, more often than is talked about, rape victims are commonly disposed of after service. That way, no charges can be filed because no witnesses can be found.

The Brothers walked away reluctantly. On their way into the darkness, the girls could hear the Brothers' promises of torture and coming misery.

When they were finally gone, Juanita walked over to Paige. "Miss Paige... you call Border Policia."

Paige called the Border Patrol and the sheriff's office. It only took a few hours for them to round up all the Brothers. As a group, you tend to slow everyone down when one leg has a bullet hole and another leg is dog bitten. It took longer for the sheriff's office to get statements from everyone, both in English and Spanish.

When I rounded the corner in my patrol car, I almost had a heart attack. There were cop cars and Border Patrol vehicles all around my house. As soon as I got out of the car, the first thing the other deputies did was assure me that Paige was all right. That was good to hear, but not enough.

I caught myself holding my breath again as I walked through the crowd of officers on my porch. Finally, I walked through the front door and saw Paige sitting in one of the chairs while talking to the sheriff. About the same time I walked in, she noticed me and smiled. She was just as beautiful as I had left her.

The story alone was so exciting that it made me a nervous shaking wreck for a month. Although it was the nature of my profession to be the middle of the action, Paige had managed to live more in a twelve-hour period than I had during our entire stay in South Texas.

Juanita, Silvia, and Maria became lifelong friends with Paige. Paige helped every one of them with their immigration paperwork and to this day they are all regular visitors. They became family.

One night while lying in bed, I was awakened by laughter. It was Paige laughing in her sleep. She was so loud, she woke both of us up. I had to ask if she could remember what in her dream was so funny. She said it was about Nail and how he was chasing a javelina through the middle of the house while she was trying to cook breakfast.

Well, you know, it was a dream.

After she quit laughing and she was still awake, I asked, "Paige. I know it's been rough on you, being here and all... you ever have any thoughts about leaving anymore?"

"Not a chance, Henry." She told me with certainty. "I'm here to stay."

I guess a few moments had passed and I had drifted back into sleep land when she woke me up with her own question. "Henry?"

"Yes, sweetheart?"

"You would consult with me before you brought a live javelina into the house, wouldn't you?"

"Yes. Yes, I would."

The Fishing Trip

I sat on the couch while still in my Batman underwear, glued to the fishing show on TV. Chad Dorsalfinn, a professional TV fisherman, was showing the world how to catch a record-breaking bass on a spotted swamp frog. He just threw the squirming frog overboard and let the frog do all the work. As soon as the critter hit the top of the water, it started frog stroking for its life towards the bank. Mr. Frog never made it.

Chad Dorsalfinn never seemed very excited about the catch as he reeled him into the boat. He just grabbed that monster bass by the bottom lip and held him up for the camera. Then came his usual worthless and aggravating commentary that he always gave after a catch, "This bass lived in the water... he ate my frog... I will now release him back into the wild... I need another frog."

Yeah, right. I didn't buy it. There was nothing special about that fish. It was the same commentary crap that he said about every fish.

I thought Dorsal-brain was making way more money than what he deserved. And he looked too pretty. His clothes were too neat and his mirrored sunglasses made him look like a playboy racecar driver. I wanted to see a real man, like myself, struggle to pull a leviathan from the depths, growl like a barbarian, and then throw that fish in the ice chest for a future fish fry—like a man.

"Arturo! What in the living hell?" my wife shouted at me as she stood there with her hands on her hips.

She made me jump; I could see she was very displeased. "Chad Dorsalfinn caught a fish on a frog," I said to her, as milk and cornflakes dribbled down my Batman shirt and onto the couch.

"You're making a mess," she continued.

"Sorry, Honey. I think there's something wrong with this fork."

She grabbed my fork from me, "Give me that... eating cereal and milk with a fork? Of all the things," then walked into the kitchen.

"All the spoons were dirty," I tried to explain.

I'll be the first one to admit that my wife, Vikki, is the greatest. She brought order to the house. In fact, I would go so far to say that she tolerated me, despite all my faults.

We first met when she was running her father's big tire store in Seguin. When I laid eyes on her for the first time, I was totally smitten by her looks. Every time I got around her I literally forgot how to talk. All I could manage to do was mumble.

I knew I wasn't getting anywhere with Vikki, so one afternoon, after regrouping my wits by buying a whole set of tires and then shocks, I finally worked up the courage to ask her out. Six months later we were married and I've never driven on bad tires since.

Vikki's parents were originally from Mexico. She grew up with three brothers. All of them spoke Spanish. At age twenty she was managing the office of the tire shop. That's where she learned how to handle men and keep order around the shop. Whether it was respect or fear is for anybody to guess. All I know is that it worked.

As for me, I was a salesman in the fishing department of a sporting goods store. I had a daily routine of trying to convince customers to buy things they didn't need. And it all started with a whopper fish story.

Some people called it good salesmanship. I called it the psychological approach to the gullible. If I could transport a customer's imagination into a mosquito-infested fantasyland that was full of fish, I'd be half way to a sale. But I've never been pushy.

It's hard to say no when there's stuffed fish starring at you in sexy poses from the walls of the store. To close the sale, I'd usually tell them something like, my wife is a Garcia and my dog's name is Shimano. That's when they'd start throwing credit cards at me. That's what I did, every day. I enticed my customers to want it.

That's about as pushy as I got. Vikki has enough of that dominant gene for the both of us.

You might think that the last thing on my mind would be fishing when

I got off work, but you'd be wrong. I'm an avid fisherman who's always looking for the opportunity.

When the following spring came around, Vikki and I packed up our things and headed to Port Aransas on the Gulf Coast. We both needed some rest and relaxation from work. Vikki was going to lay in the sun and read a book. I was going to declare war on insolent fish that needed to be eaten.

I wanted to do some night fishing for speckled trout and redfish, and I knew exactly the spot. It was going to be the local boat docks where the shrimp boats tied up. At night, the hanging streetlights would come on over the water and attract all kinds of bait fish, that in turn brought in the bigger fish.

We arrived early at the motel while it was still daylight. My plan was to spend some time with Vikki until it got dark, but there was a problem that had hit me on the way to Port Aransas. I had developed a headache and it was getting worse by the minute.

To pass the time, Vikki and I took a couple's walk on the beach then went back to the motel. With nothing much to do until the sun went down, we decided to play some cards at the dining room table to pass the time.

Vikki didn't know how to play poker, so we played the appropriate game of Go Fish. After three hands I realized that I wasn't having any fun. My headache was pounding away. I opened a beer and washed two aspirin down, but it didn't seem to have any affect. My head was now killing me and I told her so. That's when Vikki had an idea.

"Arturo. Wait here. I've got something that might help," she said.

"I'll try anything. This thing is making me nauseous," I told her.

Vikki pulled out a small dark colored bottle from her purse, opened it, and dribbled some into my half-full beer. I downed it without asking any questions.

"What is it?" I asked after I finished.

"I'm not really sure," she replied. "Maria gave it to me. It's supposed to be good for sinus problems and headaches—an old Mexican recipe potion kind of a thing."

"Have you tried it?" I asked.

"No. But I haven't had a headache either."

We played a few more hands of cards. Time passed and nothing had changed. In fact, my headache was much worse. It felt like my pounding head was trying to push my eyeballs out of their sockets with every heartbeat. Everything I looked at developed a weird looking halo around it and I was losing my color perception. I was having trouble telling the red suits from the black suits.

So with one small act to try to lessen the pain, I held my cards up to my face because the light was hurting my eyes. It didn't work, so I closed my eyes momentarily and softly moaned.

Vikki had to have heard me moan. After all, I was right in front of her, but I don't seem to remember if she said anything. In fact, the only thing that I can remember is thinking that I must be having a stroke.

Then from behind my hand of cards I forced myself to peek out, and I was absolutely stunned at what I saw. Vikki was cheating at cards. That's right, I caught her trying to pull a fast one on me. Her own husband!

I jumped to my feet, "Vikki! You're cheating!"

"What? You're out of your damn mind!" she barked at me like a veteran barfly.

That did not sound like her. I didn't have time to wonder where that strange voice of hers came from, because she jumped out of her chair, threw down her cards, and put up her fist.

"I ain't believing this shit," I thought to myself, looking at her surrounded by that halo. "My own sweet wife. A card cheater?"

"You're a *pendejo!*" she yelled.

The next thing happened so fast I still have trouble comprehending it. Vikki and I have never been physical with each other before, but she took a swing at me and missed.

Without thinking, I returned fire, slapping her across the face; she went straight down. As soon as she hit the floor, I regretted it. That was totally unlike me in character and temperament.

Did I say I regretted it? You have no idea how bad I did. Not because her brothers would kick my ass—'cause they would. Not because I would be labeled a wife beater—'cause I would. No, I feared she would never see me as her loving husband again. So as fast as she hit the floor, I jumped on the apology train. I knew I had to make things right again, and fast.

But, oh no! Fate wasn't about to let me off that easy because the story didn't end there. It had just started. I was about to be dragged through the pits of hell by my testicles for my penitence. I had set the stage for a marathon session of sexual abuse. My own.

The way I figured it was like this: When I slapped Vikki across the face, somehow I disconnected the logical part of her brain. The lobe of the brain that makes a person capable of reasoning, whatever it's called, was gone in an instant. At the same time, I unwittingly engaged the libido lobe of her brain, and I evidently opened up all the valves. That's right my friends, my wife had turned into a full-fledged, every man's nightmare, nymphomaniac with a hyperdrive.

I reached down to pick her up and tried to immediately make amends, "Oh my god, Vikki. I don't know why I did that."

As she looked at me with tear-filled eyes, she slowly stood up, "You hit me."

I felt terrible. All I could do was stand there with my mouth hanging open, "I don't know why."

"You know that I love you, right?" she asked me.

We just stood there for a moment, looking at each other. Of course my head was still pounding away to the point that my vision had turned off all the color. Everything was in black and white like an old movie and the halo of pain was worse.

Completely unexpectedly, Vikki lovingly grabbed me by the hand and led me into the bedroom. I don't know how she turned her attitude around so fast, but she wanted makeup sex.

Even though I wasn't exactly in the mood after the incident, I figured it was my duty to be a good husband and redeem my status.

I did my manly duties, several times.

When we finished, the bed looked like two wet pigs had been wrestling on the sheets. The lamp was also knocked off the end table.

Like any good fisherman, I was aware of where the sun was and how much time I had. It was a little early, so I still had enough time to get ready. I casually sat down and started to put on my boots, when Vikki walked up to me wearing only her sexy underwear and wanted me to go back in the bedroom for another go-round.

I figured, "Oh what the hell. I think I've got one more in me."

Afterwards, the top mattress was hanging off the box springs, the other lamp was on the floor, and I noticed the air conditioning unit was having a hard time keeping the place cool.

During a break, I went to the bathroom, turned on the faucet, and sucked down a quart of water. My body was telling me that I was getting dehydrated. I needed water and probably a shot of electrolytes. But as it turned out, my manly duties weren't finished yet.

Somehow Vikki enticed me to the bedroom for a third time.

"She's got to be kidding?" I thought to myself. "If I don't get out of here soon, she's going to drain me of all my energy to fish. It's almost time to go."

I soon forgot all about my headache because the rest of my body was in pain. Some places on me were on the verge of bleeding. It wasn't fun anymore, and she was getting more freaky as the minutes passed. Her energy level increased out of who knows where and her voice became deep and frightening. I was trying to give up and cry 'uncle,' but she wouldn't let me. She was now demanding that I perform again.

"You've got to be kidding, right?" I asked her.

She didn't have to answer. I knew exactly what she was thinking. Especially since her frizzled hair was covering her eyes when she growled at me like a mad dog. All that ran through my head was, "This redemption shit is going to kill me." The thought of fishing was now being replaced by a visit to the emergency room.

Shortly thereafter, I found myself laying on my back, drenched in sweat, and panting like I had run a mile through a swamp. As bad as my eyesight had become, I could barely make out Vikki's silhouette on top of me, grunting and clawing in the air like she was some kind of a sex-starved demon, trying to drag my body and my soul to a hellacious abyss. That's when it occurred to me—I didn't need a paramedic anymore. I needed an exorcist.

Finally she passed out with her arms laying over me. I knew that was my chance to slip away without being detected. It wasn't easy, but I managed to slide out of bed without waking her.

Vikki was still asleep when I quietly put on my clothes in the living room. Every move I made was with precision and stealth. I couldn't afford for Vikki to wake up. If she did, I might be forced to perform again and I was convinced that the next time would put me in a wheelchair.

There was only one obstacle to overcome before I made it to the front door. The bedroom door was open and the light was on in the kitchen. If I walked in front of the door, the sudden light or sound change could wake her, and I couldn't take that chance. So I got on my belly and low-crawled past the bedroom door like a navy seal. I would crawl a few inches, then quietly slide my tackle box forward, then gently move my fishing rod forward. I repeated this over and over again until I finally reached the front door.

Right before I stood up, something grabbed me by the leg. I immediately stiffened my body in defense and slowly turned around. It was my beloved Vikki, the sex demon from hell.

"Hey, lover boy," she beckoned me. "Come back to bed."

I was spent, like the last coin in an arcade. I knew that this was the end for me if I was forced to go another round.

All I could seem to do was bury my nose in the carpet and close my eyes. "Oh, no! Not again! I just can't do it!" I whimpered pathetically into the shag.

"Well then don't," I heard Vikki's voice say. "Nobody's forcing you to bet... or draw a card."

What she said didn't make any sense, so I slowly opened my eyes, and to my surprise I found myself sitting back at the dining room table playing the game of Go Fish again. This was right where I left off. The halo was gone. I could see colors again. That was exactly where things had gone haywire. Wherever I had been, I was now back.

As I gazed at Vikki, now my angel wife, she placed her card hand face down on the table and asked me, "How's your head?"

Once I thought about it, I realized my headache was gone. "Better. I think it's gone... of course it seems I had to take a trip to get here."

"I'll never understand the mysteries that float through a *gringo's* head," she told me as she smiled. "You better get ready to fish. It's nearly dark."

I had been on the runaway train of hallucinations. It's not something I would recommend to anyone for any reason.

So what's the moral of the story? It's not, "never hit your wife." That goes without saying. The moral of the story is "never mix your peyote with beer." That is, unless you fancy being held hostage by a sex demon, stripped of your honor, sexually tortured, deprived of water, and drained of your bodily fluids.

When he was ten years old, Mike Lowrie and his younger brother ran away from home, not with the intent to join the circus, but for the adventure. That's how it all started.

Born and raised in Texas, he grew up in the region of East Texas that included cotton fields and the famed piney woods of the Nacogdoches area. He spent his boy-hood in a rural life, hunting, fishing and exploring. In 1972, he moved to San Antonio, where he graduated from John Marshall High School and then joined the U.S. Army. He spent a total of four years as a military policeman, then later, ten years in the U.S. Coast Guard Reserve.

He attended Sam Houston State University in Huntsville and the University of Texas in San Antonio. In 1985, Mike joined *Buffalo Bill's Wild West Show* as a trick roper and horse trainer. In 1986, he was hired as an assistant wagon master for the *Texas Wagon Train Sesquicentennial Celebration*.

As a civilian he worked as a cowboy, oilfield roughneck, truckdriver, lawman and owned and ran his own construction business for over twenty years.

Now retired and living in Bandera County, Mike Lowrie writes books, incorporating his experiences into stories that take place mostly in Texas and from all walks of life.

www.ingramcontent.com/pod-product-compliance
Lightning Source LLC
Chambersburg PA
CBHW030808190726
48285CB00003B/1086